John Creasey – Master Storyteller

Born in Surrey, England in 1908 into a poor family in which there were nine children, John Creasey grew up to be a true master story teller and international sensation. His more than 600 crime, mystery and thriller titles have now sold 80 million copies in 25 languages. These include many popular series such as *Gideon of Scotland Yard, The Toff, Dr Palfrey* and *The Baron*.

Creasy wrote under many pseudonyms, explaining that booksellers had complained he totally dominated the 'C' section in stores. They included:

Gordon Ashe, M E Cooke, Norman Deane, Robert Caine Frazer, Patrick Gill, Michael Halliday, Charles Hogarth, Brian Hope, Colin Hughes, Kyle Hunt, Abel Mann, Peter Manton, J J Marric, Richard Martin, Rodney Mattheson, Anthony Morton and *Jeremy York*.

Never one to sit still, Creasey had a strong social conscience, and stood for Parliament several times, along with founding the One Party Alliance which promoted the idea of government by a coalition of the best minds from across the political spectrum.

He also founded the British Crime Writers' Association, which to this day celebrates outstanding crime writing. The Mystery Writers of America bestowed upon him the Edgar Award for best novel and then in 1969 the ultimate Grand Master Award. John Creasey's stories are as compelling today as ever.

DOCTOR PALFREY SERIES

The Famine

John Creasey

HOUSE OF
STRATUS

This edition published in 2009 by House of Stratus, an imprint of
Stratus Books Ltd., Lisandra House, Fore Street,
Looe, Cornwall, PL13 1AD, U.K.
www.houseofstratus.com

Typeset by House of Stratus.

A catalogue record for this book is available from the British Library
and the Library of Congress.

ISBN 07551-1770-0
EAN 978-07551-1770-3

FOREWORD

The main task of a writer of thrillers is to entertain rather than to instruct. Such instruction as occurs is usually incidental – properly vague in such subjects as breaking into safes, though sometimes usefully detailed in respect of antidotes to poisons or methods of immobilising cars. Nevertheless, any effective form of literature is extremely good at conveying and popularising new ideas. It is most encouraging to me as a scientist to see the excellent piece of entertainment which Mr. Creasey has written around a most important idea derived from his interest in the Family Planning Movement.

This idea, that a steadily multiplying population must eventually out run its resources, however large these may be, is obvious enough to the mathematician who deals in exponentials but is evidently not yet clear to those who hope to deal with human expansion by food production alone. Although there are doubtless details at which a pedant might cavil, the book is good science fiction in that the Lozi do not break any major scientific laws – and are not biologically nearly so difficult to accept as the giants in that recognised classic, H. G. Wells' *Food for the Gods.*

J. H. Fremlin
Professor of Applied Radioactivity,
The University of Birmingham, England

The problem of the starving millions has been stated, overstated and understated over many years. "The next 24 to 28 years are going to be the most critical", Dr. Binay Sen, director-general of the United Nations Food and Agriculture Organization, said in New York last night. He gave this warning: "If the rate of food production cannot be significantly increased, we must be prepared for the four horsemen of the Apocalypse." It is against this background that the Indicative World Plan for Agricultural Development is now being prepared by the F.A.O., of which *The Times* is today able to publish exclusively a summary of the first progress report.

From *The Times,* Wednesday, 19th October, 1966.

Chapter One

THE MAN WHO WAS AFRAID
OF 'RABBITS'

Neil Anderson was not a particularly big man, nor especially tall, although, as he walked along the English country lane, his physical strength and fitness were apparent. The woman sitting in the driving-seat of the old Hillman station wagon, parked beneath the shade of a big oak tree, saw this with approval. As he drew near, she noticed that he was good-looking, too, and she wondered why he was walking, where he was going and whether he would stop to pass the time of day. Across the field of wind- and storm-flattened barley, her husband had been working with a combine-harvester machine. Now it was nearly six o'clock, and she had come to pick him up.

The man drew nearer, and smiled. She smiled back at him, with a warmth which was natural to her.

Anderson stopped by the open car window.

She saw that he was preoccupied. Saw too that there was anxiety, perhaps even fear, in his glance as he looked about him.

"Forgive me for asking, but have you been here long?" She noticed that his voice held a slightly foreign inflection.

"Ten minutes or so," she answered, softening the bluntness of the words by adding: "I'm waiting for my husband."

"I see. Have you seen anything unusual?"

She liked the way he spoke as well as the way he looked, yet she was sure that he was a man afraid. Her husband regarded her as the most matter-of-fact person he knew, and indeed she was, but owned qualities of understanding and insight not always recognised.

"No. Everything is normal," she answered.

He insisted. "In the field, perhaps? Or beneath the tree when you pulled under it?"

"All I've seen are two rabbits, some sparrows, a pair of crows and a cock pheasant," she answered reassuringly. "They're not very unusual."

His eyes were very still, questioning.

"Rabbits?" he repeated sharply.

"Two." She pointed along the road towards the five-barred gate. "They bobbed out of the grass and back again, just after I came. Have you a rabbit-pie in mind?"

"No." His voice sounded impatient. "*How* many rabbits, did you say?"

Why was he so interested in the rabbits?

"Two."

"Could you show me exactly where you saw them?"

Why on earth was a foreigner walking along a country lane so interested in rabbits? For their skins? She resisted the temptation to ask him, and pointed towards the five-barred gate through which her husband, David, had taken his chattering machine. The gate was closed; whether cattle were in a field or not, he always closed the gate.

"Along there," said Betty Fordham.

Solemnly, the man said "Thank you", and raised his hat. Puzzled and curious, yet sympathetic towards him, she watched him approach the gate. The only sounds were the trilling of birds, the whispering of wind over the corn, the clanking of the combine-harvester machine. Suddenly Betty realised the stealth of the stranger's footsteps; as he drew nearer the gate, he appeared to be crouching, peering cautiously ahead – almost as if he were afraid of what he might see.

"What on earth's the matter with him?" Betty asked herself, uneasiness, even suspicion, springing to mind. Could he have escaped from a home?

Recollection of his direct glance, and the utter lack of personal interest she read in it, sobered her. Nevertheless his behaviour had not, from the first, been entirely normal. He was bending down with elaborate caution, scanning the ground near the gate, the rain-washed grass starred with the hoof marks of cattle, flattened with tyre tracks under feathery wisps of hay. No detective could have inspected the ground more closely.

Detective? Could that be ...

Suddenly he started back so suddenly that the violence of the movement shocked her. He almost fell. At the same moment, a rabbit *leapt* at him. The attack had all the desperation of a hunger-driven rat in its raw ferocity, as the animal leapt straight at his throat.

Betty Fordham sat frozen to the car seat.

The man flung up his arms to defend himself, tore wildly at the rabbit, caught it and hurled it away. The small body went flying over the gate. The man staggered backwards, patches of bright red streaking his hands. Recovering his balance, he stood motionless, staring down, as if expecting the rabbit to return to the attack.

It was fantastic! A rabbit ...

Suddenly the man swung round and ran towards Betty, and as he did so she saw three things at the same instant – several more rabbits, bounding towards him, blood on his hands and neck, and terror in his eyes. All at once she realised that he was trying desperately to reach her before the rabbits caught up with him, that he saw the car as sanctuary. Now almost as intensely involved as he, she leaned forward and flung the door open a split second before the man reached it. Three rabbits were close behind him, one made a fierce bound, and bit at his ankle. He kicked it off, and scrambled into the car, slamming the door.

She heard a squeak, as of pain.

"Windows!" he gasped. "Windows! *Keep them out.*"

Her window was wide open, and she saw two rabbits – *rabbits!* – spring towards it. Seized by his fear, she snatched at the handle and wound it desperately, hearing scratching sounds at the door. In the back, the man sat gasping and shivering, slowly bleeding. Betty twisted round in her seat, and saw the ugliness of the gashes in his throat, and on the backs of his hands.

"Telephone," he muttered. "Must reach a telephone."

The nearest was at the Goose Inn, at the cross-roads a mile along the lane.

"Telephone. Please hurry."

He was pressing against the wound in his neck in an endeavour to staunch the flow of blood. His eyes were staring. Again a fleeting, fearful thought crossed her mind: That he was mad. Even as she thought this, she was switching on the ignition and pulling the self-starter. Mad or not, he needed a doctor. She mustn't lose a moment getting to the telephone. She started off, doing everything quickly and with the good driver's expertise, although she was still so horrified that she had not said a word. Staring ahead through the windscreen, she saw no rabbits.

They had been rabbits, and yet there had been something different about their appearance as well as about their behaviour. She carried the picture of what she had witnessed in her mind like a scene from a film, a confused medley of feverish movement and activity, of scratching paws, of lips drawn back . . .

Lips! Rabbits didn't have lips like human beings, but these had. Or was it an hallucination? Had she really seen lips and faces which were more like tiny human faces than the faces of rabbits?

The man began to speak in a slow measured voice: "Tell the police they must inform Dr. Palfrey. Please understand. Dr. Palfrey. Say I did not know they were deadly – but I saw one kill a dog. After that I was afraid. You must understand. Dr. *Palfrey*. Please say that name."

She did not turn round, but repeated: "Dr. Palfrey. P-A-L-F-R-E-Y."

"Good," he said, and seemed to sigh.

Betty could not think clearly, and the speed at which she drove blurred vision of the leafy hawthorn hedge on either side, fields, sharp-speared grass, birds, even the sky and the far-off hills. The car was hurtling along, and suddenly she realised that she was

4

panic-stricken; this furious speed was a measure of the fear this man, and the incident, had put into her.

She slowed down as the road surface improved, until at last the Goose Inn showed up above the hedge, angled against the sky, slates and grey stone dark even in the sun which glinted on the windows and was absorbed by the roofs of two long sheds. No cars were outside. The telephone poles, stretching across the countryside like matchsticks strung together with cotton and stuck in bright green plasticine, made her think of the man in the back of her car, and the husky way he had muttered: *"Telephone. Telephone."* She turned her head.

"Oh, no!" she gasped.

He was slumped back in a corner, hands loosened as those of a doll, mouth slack, eyes staring. After the first shock, she knew the truth. The man was dead. Blood glistened bright red, on his neck. She drove on mechanically, drawing nearer the ugly, solitary inn. She put her hand on the horn, and the harsh stridency of its note slashed the silence. No one stirred.

She got out of the car slowly, braced herself, and opened the back door, stretching out her hand to feel the other's pulse, yet quite sure there would be no movement.

A man appeared at the side door of the Goose Inn – Jacob Gosling, the fifth in his line to own the inn, which had been named by his great, great grandfather. He was short, dark, saturnine, a man whom no one liked yet whom no one had cause to dislike.

"What is it?" he called in his hard voice.

"Come here, Jake. Hurry!" she pleaded.

He came with his slow, deliberate, countryman's movement. She drew back from the man whose pulse did not beat; he had died as a stuck pig might die, and yet – had there been so much bleeding? Drawing away, she saw reddish-brown marks on the lower part of the window, and realised that they were figures; numbers.

Telephone ...

Jake's footsteps grated on the loose gravel, as he reached her side.

"What's the matter, Betty?" He peered into the car, and his tone and manner changed abruptly. "My God, what's happened?"

Rabbits had attacked the man. It was unbelievable.

"I—I don't know. He was by the big oak. He—he wanted to telephone." Betty Fordham paused between each word, finding them difficult to utter. "Do you see—that number?" She pointed.

Jake stared, hooded eyes wide open, trap of a mouth, for once uncertain.

"That's S1234X," he said. "Ess, one, two, three, four, ex. *Ess.*"

"Salisbury?"

"Southampton?"

"Is it a London number?"

"Or Shaftesbury?"

"Jake." Betty said urgently. "I've been scared out of my wits. Have you—have you ever seen a ferret attack a rabbit?"

"What a daft question. A thousand times."

"A *rabbit* attacked this man."

Jacob Gosling's eyelids dropped over the questioning brightness of his grey eyes, his mouth became a trap again. He did not comment, but she knew that what she said had been registered as the raving of a hysterical woman. *Was* it? If the body of the man had not been in the car, she might have thought that something had indeed turned her mind. But the body was irrefutably there. Acutely conscious of Jacob's scepticism, she said nervously: "Will you try these numbers?"

"I ought to call a doctor—and the police. The police," Jacob Gosling repeated, as if that were a new and important idea. "It's a matter for the police. You know that, surely."

"It would be half-an-hour before anyone got here!"

"They could telephone this number," Jacob remarked, and she could tell by the set of his mouth and chin that his mind was made up. "We'll leave the man in the car. I'll not touch him until the police arrive." Nothing would shift him from that decision now that it was made, but he knew only what she had told him. He took her arm and led her towards the Goose Inn, firm, determined, almost kindly. The late afternoon sun was warm. In an hour the first customers would come to the inn.

6

"Jake, listen to me."

"I'll listen while I'm on the telephone."

"Jake, rabbits did attack him."

"Yes, yes, you "told me," he said, too easily, too soothingly.

"Jake, never mind what you believe. Tell the police to send for a Dr. Palfrey. And—and tell them that rabbits with men's faces killed this stranger. Jake, *please*."

They were in a dark, narrow passage, with an open door at the far end, and a telephone fastened by a bracket to the wall.

"I'll tell them," he promised. "What name did you say?"

"Palfrey. Dr. Palfrey."

"Right then. Now you go and sit down." One door led to the saloon bar, comfortable with red-leather upholstered chairs and glass-topped tables, brass beer handles bright as polished gold, bottles glistening behind the bar. "Help yourself to what you fancy," he invited.

She did not feel like drinking. There was something on her mind, a forgotten thing, teasing, harassing. She dropped into a chair as Jake stood, with his back to her, dialling. What had she forgotten?

Jake said: "It's Jacob Gosling of the Goose Inn speaking ... Is the inspector there ... Yes, he'll do ... sergeant, this is Gosling of the Goose Inn ... I have to report a crime ... Well, a death ... A Mrs. Fordham, wife of a farmer who ... Betty Fordham, yes ... She has just come in with a dead man in the back of her car ... Yes, sergeant, I said a dead man ... She states a rabbit attacked him ... Yes, I did say rabbit ... I'm only telling you what she told me, I'm not an eye witness ... He asked for a telephone before he died, and wrote a number on the window of the car ... in blood. And he wants a Dr. Palfrey to be informed. Palfrey." All this time, Jacob's voice had been pitched at the same level, and even the words 'In blood' came out matter-of-factly. It held the monotony of a gramophone record.

"The first letter was S—yes, ess ... then one, two, three, four, ex—"

He broke off. From his attitude, the very movement of his broad shoulders and solid figure, the woman knew he had received a shock. When he spoke again, his voice was pitched on a higher key.

"That's right, ess, one, two, three, four, ex written in blood ... Yes ... She was by herself, as far as I know ... Yes, the big oak tree in Duck Lane ... on the way to Fordham's Farm ..."

Dave! Dave was in that field. That was what she had forgotten – her husband.

Betty sprang up from the chair, a vivid mental picture of the leaping 'rabbits' with their sharp teeth and their fury, flashed before her as she realised that Dave might be attacked. At all costs he must be warned. She ran into the passage as Jacob said: "Yes, I'll wait for you. Don't be too long."

She was tugging at his shoulder before he put the receiver down, her face alive with alarm and concern.

"Dave's out in that field!" she cried. "I must go and get him. He's expecting me, he'll be waiting for me, just where it happened. But I can't go alone, please don't let me go alone!"

The hard, hooded eyes sharpened, the trap of a mouth set for a moment, then relaxed.

"We've got to wait for the police," he said with mild obstinacy. "There's nothing more to it. We've got to wait for the police."

Chapter Two

THE MAN WHO FELT LIKE GULLIVER

David Fordham was hot, tired, satisfied, and just a little bit puzzled. He had done more work, single-handed, than he had expected, the storm damage had been isolated in one corner of the field, and if the weather held, he would get it finished tomorrow. He climbed down from the big, clumsy-looking machine which did the work of so many men, wiped his forehead, wished he had some cold tea left, but knew Betty would have a bottle of something with her. Betty the Reliable, who anticipated his every need. Bless her! He pulled a plastic cover over the vulnerable parts of the combine-harvester, tied them into position over the wheels, and turned to walk away.

He went two or three steps, and stopped, for straight ahead was a faint, narrow track through the waist-high barley. He did not recognise it as the track of any familiar animal. Rabbits, mice, rats, voles and foxes, left little sign of passing; cats left much more. Hares seldom came into such a field, and if there had been any recent incursion, he would have seen the tell-tale signs; he was as sure as a countryman could be that there had been none.

Then what, or who, had made these tracks?

There were three lines, thrown into relief by the slanting rays of the sun; all leading to the big oak where Betty would be waiting. He could see the top of it, a dark mass of foliage, about a quarter-of-a-mile away.

The most puzzling thing was not the tracks in themselves, but the fact that they had not been here half-an-hour ago. He himself had driven the combine-harvester past this very spot, and could not have missed such signs.

Nor did the fact that they started ten yards or so inside the uncut barley now escape him. There was a little stretch of grain through which he had walked, picking his way carefully; and the three tracks started, mysteriously, out of nowhere. He had intended to walk across the patch already cut, and then along the edge of the field, but now the tracks so interested and puzzled him that he was tempted to follow them. Comparatively little damage had as yet been done, but he was likely to cause more; that was the only reason for his hesitation.

He began to move forward.

Almost at the same moment that he did so, he heard behind him the harsh jangling of collapsing metal. He spun round. There, only a few yards away, the combine-harvester was lurching to one side, already the front wheels had sunk a foot or more into the solid ground. Utterly astounded, Dave Fordham stood and gaped.

There was nothing he could do to stop the fall. The machine, moving heavily, almost majestically, like a great ship slowly submerging, gradually settled down until the front was out of sight, and the back poked starkly into the air, the wheels still above ground.

Fordham's first thought was of a land subsidence. There had been accounts of one a few months before at the site of an old Roman burial ground near Salisbury. Uncharted burial grounds were suspected to be in the neighbourhood, but he knew of none here near Tidford. And he and his family had worked this field for thirty-odd years, and every kind of machine had been driven over it. Moreover, at one time it had been used for tank training; any underground earthworks or caves could hardly have remained undiscovered.

He began to move forward, his mind working fast but confusedly, still hardly able to believe the truth. The machine which he had covered up with such care was now standing drunkenly on ground which had sunk at least three feet. He paused momentarily before taking each step, for he was a powerful man, very heavy for his height, and if he trod on a weak spot, he might fall. The ground seemed firm enough, but he did not allow himself to be lured into a false sense of security.

The metal was still groaning, and a scattering of rooks, feasting on the ears left over by the harvester, rose high, cawing and croaking in their alarm. Gradually, they began to settle again.

Fordham heard other, different, noises nearby, like and unlike the sound of voices. Yet no one was in sight, and he could hear no one approaching. The voices, and shrill unspecified squeals, seemed to be coming from beneath him – or beneath the useless machine. Mystification at the damage, its effect on tomorrow's harvesting, and the utter obscurity of what had happened all tended to exasperate him. Some bloody young fools digging for bones! He would like to tan their hides.

He saw something move, close to the side of the nearest wheel. It was like a child, a minute child – or a dwarf. Certainly it looked human, although so small. It appeared only for a moment, then vanished. Fordham had not caught sight of its face, only the top of a head, and the curve of a tiny body. Like his wife, although for a very different reason, he wondered if this were an hallucination, and he was seeing things which were not there.

The squealing continued.

He thought automatically: I must help them. My God, there are a lot of kids under there! He forgot the risk of treading on hollow ground, felt his right foot break through the crust of stubble-covered earth, tried to save himself and failed. Arms waving, a strange dread tearing at his heart, he dropped downwards.

The fall was not far. When he came to rest, he was about waist deep in earth; he could stretch out his hands and touch stubble without effort. He must get out of here; the ground beneath him seemed firm enough. But the groaning and the squealing were louder, and before he made any attempt to move he realised that they were in fact coming from beneath the earth at its normal level.

He put his arms out to haul himself up, and almost at once the earth about him collapsed beneath his weight. As it crumbled the other sounds grew louder, shriller, more piercing. Chaff from the cut grain rose, half-blinding him, increasing the feeling of nightmare. Gradually, as the dust cleared away he was able to distinguish one thing from another.

It was as if he were looking out at the after-effects of a bomb; or an earthquake. Small pieces of brick and rubble, stones and earth, were piled in a heap in front of his eyes. Hands and feet, heads and arms, of dozens of tiny people appeared everywhere. Some of the creatures were clawing at the rubble to free themselves. Hands and cheeks were streaked with blood, fear, *terror,* showed on the miniature faces.

It must be a dream, Fordham thought wildly.

He felt like Gulliver in the world of Lilliput, but Gulliver had never set eyes on such a tragedy as this. The hideous thing was the number of people beneath the debris, although the collapsed area was really quite small – not much more than the size of one of his sheds.

I must go and get help, he thought.

I don't believe I'm seeing straight. I can't be.

Then he noticed two of the midget creatures staring at him, with a glare of malevolence.

He must get away and fetch help. All of the ground couldn't be hollow. He turned from the dreadful sight, and then said aloud: "I can dig 'em out with my hands!"

The moment the thought entered his head, he began to work, and suddenly the tiny creatures seemed to realise what he was doing, and to stop struggling. He dug his hands into the rubble near one of them, eased it away, and lifted the creature out. His mind rejected the evidence of his eyes. It was like handling a doll, a beautifully made, beautifully formed doll, naked except for a loin cloth. The smooth, pale body was scratched here and there, but not seriously.

Fordham put it down very carefully on the earth at waist level.

"Take it easy," he said. "You'll be all right."

He moved to rescue another, and another; thinking stupidly: "They are men." Certainly they were perfectly formed models of grown men, handsome in a way, although their size still made him think of them as dolls. He soon had twenty or so of them free, but worse was to come, for some were buried beneath the rubble. He groped for and found one, and when he brought it out, the dirt falling from it in streams, he saw that it was dead.

He placed it on the other side, away from the living creatures. Still unable to grasp what was happening, feeling as if it were a prolonged nightmare from which at any moment he would awake, he worked mechanically. There must be as many dead, now, as living creatures. He was tiring rapidly, yet could not stop, for there was no telling how many more there might be. He bent down yet again and then saw that some of those he had rescued were also helping. They carried miniature spades, picks and shovels.

The immediate relief was so great that he hardly realised the curious fact that – they had *tools*.

They were digging a tunnel.

At first, he did not really understand why, but there was no point in trying to stop them. After a few minutes he realised there was a definite purpose in what they were doing. They were digging their way towards another chamber, working quickly but with great care.

Fordham bent down to look through the growing hole; and had a startling, overall view.

He saw rooms and passages; scrupulously laid out on the plan of a miniature house. In the rooms more of the tiny creatures were huddled. Some were male, but most female – not much more than a foot high, but with beautifully formed bodies, and long, rather wavy, hair. In one room were several such females and dozens of tinier creatures, no longer than his little finger. These were the children.

In so far as Fordham was able to think at all, he realised that this house, or apartment building, had been built from the hollowed out part of the ground, and the ground itself was the only roof. The walls of the room rose about two feet. They must have dug the cave out, then erected the wall partitions.

Those he had rescued now moved among the cowering females, apparently reassuring them, talking in low-pitched voices which had little volume or strength; attenuated as the voices from a radio in which the battery was running dry. The care lavished on their women was quite fantastic. So was the next step in this unbelievable colony. 'Men' began to climb rope ladders which hung from the ceiling, and for the first time Fordham saw that the walls and the ceiling were reinforced by bracken, corn and barley stalks, leaves and twigs, like an enormous bird's nest. The fury of activity went on for a long time, until Fordham grew tired of watching, and ran his fingers through the debris, to make sure no more creatures were buried. Satisfied, he turned away, looking repeatedly over his shoulder almost in the hope that the scene would vanish. It did not. He reached the edge of the collapsed area, close to the combine-harvester. If he climbed on that, he should be able to step off the engine on to firm earth. He was now far enough from the 'building' to be reasonably sure no further loosening of earth would occur.

He climbed on to the machine, his heart very heavy. He would have no chance, now, of getting the field harvested. One part of his mind, unable to accept the marvel of what he had seen, was turning to the disappointment of everyday life in a desperate clutch on sanity.

He stood poised on the engine, cursing and looking about him. From this height, he could see very little; just a hole like the mouth of a cave with a crust of earth on top. He pictured the bustle of activity, the checking, the care for the females and children.

"Women and children be damned!" muttered Fordham. "They're midgets!" He stepped forward. "Midgets! Don't make me laugh. They must be figments of the imagination. They can't really exist."

But the sun was warm upon him, and the barley lay in its glory to the right and left. An aeroplane hummed high in the heavens and in the distance was the spreading oak tree. These things were real. He looked down at the earth, and saw at least twenty dead, miniature bodies. *They* were real, too. It was pointless to try to fool himself – he had to get to the car, to the Goose Inn, and the phone.

No one would believe him, least of all Betty! Thought of the way she would look at him made him burst into a splutter of laughter. Betty's derisively curving lips and merry blue eyes – well, thank God she hadn't walked from the car, as she sometimes did. She could easily have broken a leg.

The ground now seemed firm enough, and he strode out more vigorously, tired, but eager to get help as quickly as possible. When he glanced behind him, he could see the half-buried combine-harvester, and the waving barley, but no other indication of his adventure at all. If he had not chanced to leave the machine at that spot, he might never have experienced it. A lot of poor little baskets would be alive, the colony – like a colony of humans – would be a bustle, all of the 'people' happy and thriving.

"People."

They couldn't be people, not in the accepted sense. What, or who, the hell were they?

He was near the five-barred gate, and the oak tree. At first he thought that Betty must have parked behind a thick hedge, but soon he realised that the car wasn't there. He was surprised. He would have expected her to come into the field, if he were late, not stay some distance off. If she'd been delayed he would have to walk to the Goose, and the prospect did not please him.

As he stepped through the gateway, he saw two rabbits.

They startled him because they were standing quite effortlessly on their hind legs. They *were* rabbits; and yet they had faces like the midget men of the field. He felt sure they were two of the colony, dressed up as rabbits in some ludicrous masquerade.

"What's going on?" he asked, and when there was no answer, he raised his voice. "What's it all about?"

As he moved forward, they leapt at him, so suddenly and with such speed that he could not even put up his arms to protect himself. He saw tiny hands thrust at him, and claws – *talons* – instead of finger-nails. On the same instant, his neck was punctured at least six times, inflicting an agonising, searing pain. He staggered, round and round in a drunken spin, until suddenly he lost all control, and fell.

As he lay dying, early lovers strolled along the narrow lanes nearby, tired labourers left the fields, birds swooped low in the warm sun to feed on the insects as they rose from leaf and twig and turf. In the thatched cottages, children played and mothers worked. Each window overlooked some peaceful English scene, offering respite for the night and promise for the morrow.

In the field, beneath the broken earth, the tiny creatures toiled on.

Chapter Three

DR. PALFREY

Dr. Stanislaus Alexander Palfrey, 'Sap' to his close friends and colleagues, waited in an underground chamber beneath the heart of London's Mayfair. Here, reinforced concrete walls, floors and ceilings, were painted in such a way as to simulate wood, marble, or Italian mosaic. The lighting was so advanced in technique that one could live in it night or day, hardly realising that the rooms were a hundred feet beneath the buildings at street level. Here, it was believed, people were safe from nuclear explosions, and radioactive air and dust, from bacteriological attack, in fact from every emergency and form of attack yet known to man. The building was invulnerable, and, if it were necessary, those living in it could exist for months, until, up on earth, men could breathe the air again without fear of the wasting diseases to which radioactivity condemned them.

This particular underground fortress, for defensively it was a fortress, had a specialised purpose. It was the headquarters of Z5. Z5 was the soubriquet given to a unique organisation first conceived by the Marquis of Brett, that remarkable man who had inspired Palfrey. Today, Z5 was sponsored by all but two of the world's established governments. Peking approved and contributed towards the substantial running costs; so did Washington. The Kremlin contributed, so did Whitehall. Israel made a generous contribution; so did the United Arab Republic. Each of these and nearly every other nation believed three things about Z5.

First, that Dr. Palfrey was the only man living who could make it fully effective, for he had won the trust of every government, even of the governments of those nations which hated each other.

Second, that Z5 was vitally necessary to a world struggling to keep the peace but so often assailed by danger created not by nations but by groups of individual monopolists, by megalomaniacs whom science had made almost as powerful as nations.

Third, that its security was of paramount importance – like its freedom of action – and that the underground headquarters in London must be as nearly invulnerable as engineering ingenuity and men of foresight could make it.

There were other equally secure, local headquarters for Z5, one in each major capital. The London nerve centre could communicate with these others very quickly, by radio of such high frequency that no one could cause interference. In this, too, all the nations co-operated, so that Z5 was indeed the nerve centre, and had an authority (but little power) unique in world history. It had become what idealists had long dreamed the United Nations should be, and the single-mindedness of Palfrey and his chief assistants strengthened its authority. No one who served Z5 pledged loyalty to his country; he or she owed their first allegiance to the world. Warring nations were at least agreed that there were some matters on which they must be united, some dangers which could only be faced if they acted together. Some of them took a great deal of convincing that such a necessity had arisen, but once convinced, they set aside national sovereignty for the period of emergency.

There had been several emergencies.

Eight years before, science distorted and misused, had threatened the world with a new *Flood,* which would have drowned all living creatures. Six years before, there had been urgent danger that all the waters of the earth would dry up in a *Drought* which no one could have survived. In these, and in others, the nations had acted in unison once assured that no one nation would benefit at their expense.

18

Dr. Palfrey's great difficulty, and greatest single cause for frustration, was with leaders of nations who were prepared to lead their people to death for a principle of only transitory value.

Obviously Palfrey was a remarkable man. Few people knew how remarkable, for not only did he direct the activities of Z5 in striving to keep the nations together under considerable stresses, but he directed a world-wide intelligence service, the sole purpose of which was to watch for, and report to him, the slightest sign of danger. There had been the threat of fire, an *Inferno* which could have reduced the world to ashes, and the threat of perpetual *Sleep*. The rumours of these dangers had come early to Palfrey, and immediately he had alerted his own agents, and the world's governments; and so saved the world from disaster.

A week ago, Palfrey had first heard of the midget creatures which were to burrow and build their own pathetic fortress beneath Dave Fordham's barley. He had talked to Neil Anderson, learning about the creatures, seen first in Sweden. Anderson had known they could be dangerous; and Anderson, like a hundred other agents commissioned to this search, had set out with instructions to catch one of the creatures alive.

Palfrey did not yet know about Anderson's death.

Anywhere in England, anywhere in the world, a call to S1234X would reach Palfrey, in his office, or his study, beneath Mayfair. Twice his headquarters had been raided, and after each raid a stronger one had been devised.

Now he sat at a very large desk of red mahogany, in a big room filled with glazed bookcases and veneered filing cabinets, all of which were fireproofed, waterproofed and virtually impervious to explosion.

Seated, he appeared slight, with rounded shoulders, not by any means the popular conception of a powerful leader; standing, he was more impressive.

The expression on his pale, ascetic face was mild and vaguely sad, an innocence accentuated by the silky fairness of his hair. He had a habit, when preoccupied, puzzled or in danger, of twisting a few strands of hair about his forehead, and eventually pressing them down in a childish curl. Those who saw him for the first time, inspired by his reputation, were not a little disappointed, overlooking the steadiness of his grey eyes, and the hint of strength at his mouth and chin.

He sat alone, that afternoon, studying three reports which had come in as a result of urgent instructions issued to agents throughout the world. The request had been simply worded:

Make most thorough investigations into any report or rumour about a race of creatures sometimes described as midgets or dwarfs, sometimes as cats, rabbits, ferrets or very big rats. Investigation should be made both in rural and urban areas. Also most thorough investigations in any reports of the loss of food in warehouses, which cannot be explained convincingly. Also, of any areas where mice, spiders, insects and small animals of all kinds appear to have been killed off. Give both matters absolute priority.

Now three reports lay before him.

One was from a big wheat warehouse in Kansas City, Missouri, U.S.A. Stocks had been raided by animals believed to be rats, later suspected to be rabbits. The investigating authorities were puzzled, for they had found no further trace of the marauders. In the area there was an unusual but welcome freedom from insects, mice, all small vermin and pests.

The second report was from Tokyo; big rice stocks near Kyoto had been devoured, and the authorities could not identify the animals concerned, although rabbits—the symbol of fertility in Japan—were suspected. Small vermin and insects had almost disappeared from that area, too.

The third report had come from the Congo; tribesmen had reported the discovery of a race of white pygmies, half animal, half man. The report had not been confirmed but the circumstantial evidence was strong. The pygmies had disappeared into the bush, but warning of them had been carried to a hundred tribes.

Palfrey's right hand strayed to his hair.

He did not yet fathom, nor even begin to suspect, the full significance of this news. It was the fact that the reports were from such widely separated parts of the world he found so disturbing.

Aloud, he said: "Southampton, England; Tokyo, Japan; Kansas City, U.S.A., and also near Brazzaville, the Congo."

He pulled gently at the strands of hair, his expression set, anxiety showing clearly. His gesture was an indication of his increasing agitation. Premonition warned him of the possible significance of the reports; such premonition was based on experience, of course, and experience told him that whenever phenomena were discovered in places so far apart, in all probability it was only a matter of time before they were found in other places; possibly in many of them.

There was something about this situation which set his nerves on edge. Even before learning of the depredations, he had been disturbed about world food supplies. Many of his agents reported low stocks due to poor harvests, and hunger and starvation were liable to drive men to desperation and so to war. The shortage of food as a consequence of the swift increase in the world's population was becoming a grave preoccupation in many countries.

Any moment now, more reports would come in with further details from countries already named. The nearest possible source was Southampton. If there was such a development he could make inquiries himself. Essentially a leader, he was frequently irked by the fact that his responsibilities kept him away from the scenes of action.

A green light glowed at one of the four telephones on his desk; this was his secretary and confidante, Joyce Morgan. He lifted the receiver.

"Yes, Joyce?"

"I've some bad news," Joyce said in the quiet unemotional voice which half prepared him for what was to come. "Neil Anderson is dead."

Palfrey unwound the strands of hair, patting them into place with unconscious deliberation. Anderson, a Swede who had seldom operated in England, had been pressed into service for this investigation. That morning, he had telephoned to say that friends in Salisbury had told him of the surprising disappearance of insects and small vermin from the Avon Valley area, and he was going to question the neighbouring farmers.

"How did he die?" Palfrey asked quietly.

"He seems to have been murdered but I don't know all the details. The police from Salisbury telephoned. He'd written our number down in blood on the window of a car."

"Blood," echoed Palfrey. "Where's the body?"

"Where it was taken, near Salisbury."

"Leave him there until I arrive," ordered Palfrey. "Ask Kenneth Campson to go down at once to do the post-mortem. Put the usual word in with Scotland Yard. What else?"

"The woman who brought him away from the place where he was killed says that he was attacked by rabbits," Joyce said, and for the first time her voice held a very slight tremor.

"Where?" asked Palfrey, but before she could answer, he went on: "Get me Joe Richardson at 10, Downing Street, and while I'm talking to him brief one of the men standing by – it doesn't matter who it is – about where this thing happened. He must take me down there at once."

Palfrey rang off, and stared straight ahead, at a portrait of the Marquis of Brett, the man who had first led Z5. Then it had been an Allied and not a world-wide concept. There were moments when Palfrey seemed to need to commune with this man who had been dead for over ten years, and this was one of those times. Palfrey felt cold, with fear. Creatures who could devour huge quantities of food, who apparently devoured all insects and small vermin, who seemed to appear in the African bush, as well as in England, who could kill so swiftly, by blood-letting – he shivered.

A blue light glowed on a telephone; this was one of the Prime Minister's personal assistants, Joe Richardson, the liaison officer between 10, Downing Street and Z5.

"What's on, Sap?" Richardson had a rather casual way of speaking as if it could really be of no importance what the conversation was about. He was a willowy young man, and on the whole likeable.

"I don't much care for the indications," Palfrey answered. "I think we might be in for a major panic."

Richardson said sceptically: "Scaremongering again."

"I hope I am. Meanwhile I think we ought to have the police and the troops of Southern Command standing by for emergency action. Better safe than sorry," Palfrey added, taking comfort in a cliché. "Will you ask the P.M. to fix this?"

"Just on your say so?"

"Yes," Palfrey said sharply. "I'll give chapter and verse if I want any action taken, but I'd like to make sure we can snap into action."

After a pause, Richardson said soberly: "I'll fix it, Sap."

"Thanks," said Palfrey.

He rang off, leaned back in his chair, and closed his eyes. Against the pinkness of the blood, seen through his eyelids, he imagined rabbits, dozens of rabbits, with fine, pointed teeth, filed like the teeth of Dracula. He shivered again, and stood up. As he passed the door of the adjoining room, he put his head round it.

"I'm off, Joyce. Who's coming with me?"

"Baretta."

"Thanks," Palfrey said. He gave her an absent-minded smile and closed the door. One of the odd things about his relationship with Joyce Morgan was that he often did not really see her. He knew she was there, dark-haired, quietly attractive, but she seldom registered on him as a woman. Once this had caused deep resentment in her; now those days had passed, though her love for him had not.

He slipped into a narrow passage and then into a lift large enough for two people only. It shot him up to one floor below ground level, and from here he walked to a flight of steps, and arrived in the busy concourse of Green Park Underground station. He walked to Dover Street, where a streamlined Allard waited, with a dark-haired, dark-eyed man at the wheel – Jim Baretta, an Italian who served Z5 with a passionate loyalty. Palfrey got in.

Baretta started off at once, speaking without glancing at his passenger.

"Joyce thinks you ought to have two more cars behind you, Sap."

"She's right," Palfrey said. "Isn't she fixing it?"

Baretta smiled. "Yes."

"Then what are we worrying about?" Palfrey sat back and closed his eyes – and again rabbits swarmed in front of his mind's eye. Rabbits. He sensed the skill with which Baretta threaded his way through the traffic, and was still sitting with his eyes closed when they reached the Embankment near Lambeth Bridge. With a minimum of delay, they went down stone steps towards a helicopter station, stepped into a two-man machine, and took off almost on the instant. As they flew over London, Palfrey looked down at the sprawling mass of chimneys which rose like cylindrical mushrooms in a spawning ground, at the occasional ugly square which towered above the slender houses. He thought, not aware of the bitter irony: *I feel like Gulliver.*

Soon, they were flying over open fields. The silver ribbon of the Thames weaved and turned among the massed green and among the red and grey and yellow of roofs. Very quickly, they came within sight of the spire of Salisbury Cathedral, skirting the lighted cross that stood out as a warning to all aircraft.

"Where are we going?" Palfrey asked Baretta.

"To a pub called the Goose Inn." Baretta answered in English so natural and colloquial it was hard to believe he had been born in Genoa. "A message has just come over the radio, Sap – from Joyce."

"Ahhh," Palfrey sighed, and the sigh was touched with fear. "More reports from overseas?"

"Yes, indeed," answered Baretta. "A warehouse in Leningrad has been eaten empty of wheat. Scores of rabbits reported to be in the vicinity. Rice fields in Southern India have been invaded by animals believed to be rabbits, the entire crop stripped, as if locusts had devoured the lot. Have you any idea what's going on?"

"Not yet," Palfrey said, and the apprehension was in his eyes as well as in his voice. "But I already know how much I dislike it. Can you sight this Goose Inn?"

Baretta pointed downwards.

On the folds of Salisbury Plain, in the midst of a flat expanse of green and yellow, gold and brown, was a solitary building, stark and unlovely, with one road sweeping past it, and two lanes converging on to it. Dotted about the fields of wheat and barley, grass and clover, were clusters of cottages, and an occasional farmhouse surrounded with the usual outbuildings. Near the Goose Inn itself were three cars, one of them carrying a sign and a spotlight.

"That's it all right," Palfrey said. "I wonder how long—"

He broke off, with a catch in his breath, and Baretta exclaimed aloud. Some distance from the Goose Inn, in a field where a huge tree stood heavy with foliage, a cloud appeared to rise out of the earth, and to spread and spread. As the helicopter moved towards it, the cloud moved in turn, across the fields towards the city of Salisbury and the cathedral's majestic spire.

Chapter Four

VIEW FROM THE AIR

Baretta, his voice edged with alarm, said: "What is it?"

"It looks like a smokescreen," Palfrey answered. He switched on the radio, already tuned in to the headquarters of Z5. "This is Palfrey," he announced, and the operator, deep beneath Mayfair, responded. "There is a cloud which could be smoke or gas, between Salisbury and the Goose Inn. It looks as if it might be intended to cover movement of some kind. It wants tracking from the air and along the ground. Alert Army and Air Force to help in keeping it in sight."

The operator said mechanically. "Message received."

"Thanks." Palfrey rang off. He glanced about him and saw another helicopter close by, identical with his own. He timed in to it. "Z5-X can you hear me.?"

"Z5-X, hearing you loud and clear."

"Do you see the patch of smoke?"

"We can see it."

"Keep flying above and behind it," Palfrey ordered. "You'll get help soon. Understood?"

"Fully understood."

Palfrey switched off, still staring at the moving patch of smoke. He had seen similar phenomena before; it was remarkable how often a smokescreen proved the best kind of concealment; one of the earliest of his investigations, into the *Mists of Fear,* had revealed that a mist, something like electoplasm, had concealed creatures no one had suspected of existing.

"Where now?" Baretta asked.

"Goose Inn."

"That smoke gives me the creeps."

"I fully sympathise."

Palfrey made himself look away from the cloud, towards the oak tree, and the fields where it had first appeared. An old machine, rather like a combine-harvester, looked as if it had fallen into some kind of earth subsidence, and he believed that the smoke had come from that very place. He scanned the field with powerful glasses, saw more evidence of the subsidence, and had a strange impression: that he could see the bodies of a dozen babies, lying side by side, close to the spot where the earth had given way.

Babies.

Then he saw a man lying on his face, strangely desolate, in the lane which led to the inn. Palfrey took it for granted, without knowing why, that the man was dead. Was that Anderson? Or was there another victim? He must find out quickly.

He saw soldiers, in twos, at various places, as if the area had been cordoned off; if it had, that was good.

Soon, the helicopter was directly over the Goose Inn. A dozen people stood about the three cars, including two uniformed policemen. Moving along the road was a white ambulance; that would be for Anderson. The years had taught Palfrey to accept the sudden death of agents as inevitable, but each one brought its own sorrow and its own crop of memories. He and Anderson had once survived deadly danger together.

Baretta landed the helicopter lightly as a feather. One of the policemen came across the field towards them, a sergeant in dark blue. He watched Palfrey closely, and waited for him to speak.

"I'm Palfrey," Palfrey said. "Have you had any more trouble?"

"I'm Sergeant Cooper, sir. Not as far as I know, sir."

Sergeant Cooper was an astute man, careful not to commit himself.

"Is an Army detail on the way?" Palfrey asked.

"Yes, sir. I've just been informed of that by radio." The statement was flat and factual, but Cooper was obviously puzzled and wary. "I've kept everyone away from the place where the man was attacked, waiting for expert opinion, sir. Mrs. Fordham whose husband is still near the spot, is very anxious to go and find if he's all right."

Palfrey thought of the body he had seen.

"You don't think it's straightforward murder, sir, do you?"

Surely that was a fool question.

"By rabbits?" Palfrey asked.

Cooper was a lean man, only a little above average height, with a leathery face deeply tanned, clear eyes, a long nose with a high bridge and pinched-in nostrils.

"Mrs. Fordham saw the man attacked. She was very frightened, sir."

"Ah. Hallucination, you think?"

"It's possible."

"No doubt it is," Palfrey said. "Cooper."

"Yes, sir."

"We might be involved in a very peculiar business indeed. A great number of people might see the same hallucinations, and if they do, rumour will spread quickly. I would rather it didn't for the time being. I don't mind the mystery of a murder, but I don't think it would be wise to say too much about rabbits. Is Mrs. Fordham likely to let her tongue run away with her?"

"I don't know her well enough to say, sir, but generally speaking she's very level-headed."

"How is she now?"

"Just getting over the shock, sir, and talking to Jacob Gosling, the innkeeper. I'm afraid there's no way of stopping wild talk about rabbits though. Several people heard her story."

"Pity," Palfrey said. "Great pity."

He approached the front of the Goose Inn, heavy hearted. Cooper would know the situation, and it had to be faced. A rumour that a man had been attacked and killed by two rabbits would now spread, but of course no one would believe it – they would assume that some creatures other than rabbits had been involved.

Wildcats? Foxes? What he needed was a story which would satisfy the local people and the newspapers, but he doubted if that was possible. Man kills rabbit, no news story. Rabbit kills man, and the story would be flashed around the globe. Until he knew much more, he did not want this spread about. Were the creatures rabbits? Were *all* of them deadly? Until he knew, until he found it impossible to avoid, he did not want terror to spread.

The ambulance pulled up.

"Which is Mrs. Fordham ?" asked Palfrey.

"The heavy woman with the green jumper," said Cooper.

'Heavy' was not a good description. Plump, perhaps, but there was a comeliness about her; a wholesomeness.

"Introduce me, please," Palfrey said.

The thing which most surprised him about Mrs. Fordham was the brightness of her eyes. Here was an intelligent woman, and he did not for one moment believe that she had imagined what she had seen. He had to take a chance on her goodwill.

"Mrs. Fordham," he said, "I am an Intelligence officer, and I'm intensely interested in your story. Will you say as little as possible about it until we've been able to talk?"

There was a hint of apprehension in the clear blue eyes.

"Perhaps I've already said too much."

"Let's hope not," Palfrey said. "It's a very serious matter indeed."

Her apprehension faded into a kind of wary appraisal, as if she could not quite make this man out; he had a very good impression of her composure.

"Have you talked to the newspapers, yet?" he asked.

"No one's been here from the Press, as far as I know," answered Mrs. Fordham.

"Good. I want to go along to the spot where you saw these rabbits," Palfrey said. "If you'll come with me, we can talk on the way. Will you?"

"I've been trying to get someone to take me there, or allow me to go," she said. "My husband will wonder what's happened to me." Again, Palfrey had a mental picture of the man lying near the big oak tree.

"Then let's go," he said.

"So you don't write me off as subject to hysteria," Mrs. Fordham remarked.

"I do not."

Mrs. Fordham gave a little shiver.

"Will you want to use my car? That's the old Hillman."

"May we?"

"I'll go and wait in it," she said. "I don't mind admitting I don't feel too good." She nodded and went off, and he felt sure she was concealing her anxiety for her husband.

The body of Neil Anderson was lifted from the ground and carried to the ambulance. Palfrey climbed inside, pulled back the covering blanket, and studied the face of his friend. He saw the incisions on the neck that had pierced the carotid artery. It might well prove that Neil had bled to death. He would soon know.

"Take him to the morgue in Salisbury," he ordered. "Mr. Gampson is on his way from London to do the autopsy."

"Very good, sir."

Palfrey left the ambulance, fully aware that everyone was watching him. Probably Cooper and the other policeman, a taller, younger man, were disappointed, for his reputation was greater than his apparent vagueness and indecision seemed to warrant. In a way, it was so. There was so much to do, in so short a time, and he alone was aware of the growing danger. One false, or ill-considered, move and the situation would be out of hand. His fear was that some vital thing would be overlooked.

Baretta was standing with the two policemen when Palfrey joined them.

"Two or three things," he said, much more briskly than before. "I'm going to the scene of the attack with Mrs. Fordham, I'd like two men within a very short distance, covering us. Sergeant, don't forget we want to play the rabbit story down. Your way's the best – let it out that you think Mrs. Fordham was overwrought. We'll have an Army detail here soon. Send it to the field by the big oak tree. Have the field surrounded, and the men at the ready. Keep in touch with our helicopters for news of the smoke – we think we saw a smokescreen, and we want to find out what movement it was intended to conceal." He turned to Cooper, with a smile. "It all sounds crazy, and that's what it may prove to be, but I'd rather be safe than sorry."

His cliché fell on fruitful ground.

"You can rely on us, sir."

"I'm sure I can," Palfrey said.

"There's just one thing, sir." Cooper was earnest.

"What's that?"

"Is there anything we can say which might explain what's on, and what all the mystery is about?" asked Cooper.

He was most astute, the kind of man Z5 could put to good use. Palfrey knew that he should have thought of this already, it should have been obvious to him, although not obvious to Cooper, who waited as if for an oracle to speak. The other people, staring, hardly seemed to move as the ambulance slid by to the noise of approaching lorries, bringing the first contingent of troops.

"Yes," Palfrey said suddenly. "Good thought – thanks. Say we're worried about a new breed of rat, which has done a lot of damage to food supplies, and might carry disease. Say it's been known in other countries and we want to make sure it doesn't spread here."

Cooper gave an appreciative smile.

"That will scare them off, sir!"

"I hope so. Jim – you deal with the military side." Baretta nodded, and Palfrey turned to Mrs. Fordham, who was sitting solidly at the wheel of her station wagon. Palfrey got in beside her, and twisted round to see the brownish message on the window written in blood. As she drove off Mrs. Fordham said abruptly: "Do you think I'm callous?"

"Farming folk are used to blood and life and death."

"Thank you, Dr. Palfrey," she said, her voice carefully held in control.

"Tell me exactly what happened, please."

She told him in surprisingly vivid detail, and Palfrey could almost see the lane and Anderson walking so warily. He was aware that Mrs. Fordham was keeping a sharp look-out; and so indeed was he, fully alive to the fact that the next yard of hedge, the next hillock, the next crop of nettles or wild parsley, could hide a watching rabbit. Every nerve was strung to breaking-point, although he tried to tell himself that such excess was ridiculous.

They turned a bend in the lane and found the oak tree straight ahead of them sturdy and strong, offering a kind of sanctuary, one side gilded by the sun, the other in deepest shadow.

Mrs. Fordham caught her breath. Palfrey glanced at her, and saw that her whole expression had changed. She had seen something which appalled her. She was staring along the lane near the gate, and he looked in the same direction. He saw the man, lying on his stomach, arms crumpled beneath him. He was a big man, wearing blue jeans which had faded almost to white, and a yellow shirt. He had reddish hair, very curly. This was the man he had seen from the helicopter, of course; whom he had kept on remembering. He had had no idea Mrs. Fordham's car would pass so close.

Now, the woman by Palfrey's side slowed down, stopped, and applied the hand brake with controlled deliberation. She said with the unnatural precision of the greatly shocked: "That's my husband. They attacked him, too. Oh God, what has come upon us?"

She began to open the door and climb out. Palfrey, too, slid out on his side, watching not only the woman but the hedgerows, even the low branches of the tree.

He looked for 'rabbits'.

And he put his hand, protectively, to his neck.

Chapter Five

THE EXODUS

All the time, Palfrey's mind was working, probing, acutely alive to the fact that there must be other aspects he had missed. He was deeply troubled by the significance of the cloud of smoke or vapour. Confident that it would be watched, and that whenever he needed to make a closer examination he could do so, he had come here with this woman, but he had warned no one of possible danger from the 'smokescreen'; that had been a mistake. He glanced behind, to see Police Sergeant Cooper's colleague, and a man he did not know, together in the police car. He beckoned. The men were so intent on the body near the gateway, that they did not notice him. He gave a hissing sound between his lips; the woman took no notice but the men looked up.

The policeman came hurrying.

"Yes, sir?"

"Have you a radio?"

"Yes, sir."

"Flash a message to your headquarters asking them – telling them – to be extremely cautious until we know the truth about the smokescreen. It could be poisonous."

"Right, sir." Unperturbed by that ominous suggestion, the policeman cast a troubled glance at Betty Fordham. She had reached the body, and stood looking down at it. Palfrey waved the men away and stepped to her side. She did not appear to notice him.

Palfrey saw the stain of blood in the earth, from the wound in the dead man's neck. He was sure of death in his own mind, but bent down and felt for the left wrist. The woman made no comment, and did not stir.

Palfrey drew back from the lifeless hand.

"Dave," Betty Fordham whispered. "Oh, Dave."

Palfrey took her arm, but she stood, as immovable as a rock.

"Dave," she repeated.

"Mrs. Fordham," Palfrey said, "we need your help more than ever."

"Help," she echoed without looking up.

"Very great help," said Palfrey. "You may have seen something which no one else in the world has seen. It's more than ever necessary for you to talk only to me, for the time being."

She didn't speak.

"Have you any children?"

Huskily, she said: "No, no children."

So, children could not comfort her, and there would be no companionship. He watched her, his mind still seeking and probing. One simple thing dropped into place. Two men had probably bled to death, as a result of wounds in the throat; so throats must be protected before any close examination of the field was made, and a warning must be flashed back. But this was not the factor that teased him, hovering on the edge of his conscious mind.

He heard a car engine, and looked up to see an army jeep with half-a-dozen men in it, approaching. A fresh-faced young lieutenant appeared to be in charge. He sprang down, glanced at the body, avoided looking at Betty Fordham and said: "What can we do, sir?"

"The vulnerable place is the throat," Palfrey said. "Everyone engaged in this affair needs throat protection – thick plastic, metal, something pliable and easy to put on and off."

"I'll report that, sir. Anything else?"

"Yes. What have you got to protect my throat now?"

The innocent-seeming brown eyes shadowed.

"Let me think a moment, please."

A tough, taut-looking corporal, approaching, said: "Sir."

"Yes, Corporal?"

"Would two army gaiters, clipped together, do the trick?"

"Would they?" the lieutenant asked Palfrey.

"Damned good idea. I'd like your men to protect themselves, by that means, and then spread out and cross this field. It should be cordoned off as soon as possible."

"Men are moving into position, sir."

That was comforting; the speed and efficiency of the army when prompt action was needed was always reassuring.

"Good." Palfrey turned to the policeman and his companion. "Will you take Mrs. Fordham to the Goose Inn?" he asked. "I'll come back to see her there as soon as I can."

"Very good," the policeman said uneasily, not sure how to deal with the woman who had been so suddenly and cruelly bereaved.

Men were busy, clipping together the wide khaki canvas gaiters that were to protect their necks. In the distance, more vehicles were in sight and soldiers were being detailed to surround the field. Palfrey was anxious to find out what had happened, but reluctant to leave the woman unsupported. There would be real danger that after the death of her husband had really struck home, she would be so bitterly hurt that she might say whatever came into her head; and who could blame her?

"Mrs. Fordham," the policeman said nervously.

She stared steadily down at her husband.

"Mrs. Fordham," Palfrey's voice was sharply authoritative.

She looked round at him.

"I want to come with you," she said simply.

The obvious thing was to say she could not; and yet she would be better with something to do than on her own, thinking, grieving. And she would recognise a 'rabbit' if one appeared. With only a moment's hesitation, Palfrey said: "That'll be a great help. Thanks." He stretched out for one of the gaiter collars, gave it to her, and went on: "Put that round your neck. How do we secure it?" he asked the corporal.

"Easy enough to adjust the buckles and straps, sir."

He was a resourceful chap, the kind of lean, leathery type who had probably seen years of service and some action.

"Good," Palfrey nodded to the policeman as the man drew nearer to the car. They waited until the gaiters had been adjusted, and Betty Fordham had made hers more comfortable. Then at Palfrey's side, she walked through the gateway, with the lieutenant, the corporal and his men behind him – at Palfrey's order.

The policeman and his companion lifted the body of Dave Fordham, and carried it to the police car. They should mark the spot where the body had lain, of course, the usual routine of investigation was essential; but the police would see to that. Palfrey walked alongside Betty Fordham across the field, taking the path already trodden by her husband. The only sound was the buzz of insects, droning in the heat, and the gentle swish of the barley as they passed. They could see nothing beyond it until they came in sight of the combine-harvester.

"It's fallen into a hole," Betty said in a strained voice.

"Yes." Palfrey was thinking of those 'babies' he had noticed from the helicopter. He scanned the land where the barley had been cut, and then saw the spot where the subsidence began. Almost at once, he saw the bodies, laid out so neatly. They were not of babies, but of midget men. As he drew near, he saw how beautifully formed each one was; and he saw, also, that each face was hairless. He did not know why that made such an impression on him, but it did. Palfrey looked at Betty Fordham, but she gave no sign of response. One of the soldiers exclaimed 'My Gawd!' No one else spoke, but all stood still, surveying the scene of destruction.

From here, they could see the 'city'.

Palfrey would never know what kind of impression that made on the others, only what effect it had on him. He was appalled. It *was* a primitive city, in miniature, the earth walls, the rooms, the separate terraces of houses like those in American Indian pueblos, the communal rooms, the communal kitchens. He judged it large enough to house not dozens but hundreds, possibly thousands, of these tiny creatures. There were beaten tracks, or roads, and 'streets'; there were tiny wheeled carts, motionless now. There were what looked like Greek or Roman amphitheatres, roughly shaped.

"My *Gawd!*" breathed the soldier, again: "It's like a huge native village."

Palfrey thought. "And they've gone, leaving their dead behind." The word which came to his mind was exodus. The creatures had suffered a major disaster, these tiny semi-human things who had lived here, possibly protected by the fur-clad 'rabbit men'. He needed no more telling what the smokescreen had meant; they had marched off under its cover. Somewhere not far away, a few miles at most, this colony of midget 'men' were still on the march.

At least, they couldn't get far, he thought.

But where would they go? Where were they heading? What would they do? Would they burrow again and try to build a new city? He could only guess, but even guessing was slow, his mind numbed by this wonder which was also horror.

As his mind cleared, he thought: I've put everything I can think of in hand. The colony would not escape of course, and that recollection reassured him at least in one way. Now he could consider the problem objectively.

Betty Fordham said unexpectedly: "It's like an earthquake."

And that indeed was what it must have seemed like to those creatures, as they died.

"And Dave did it," she said, stonily. "He didn't know they were there." She went on, her voice strengthening, warming to life. "He was the kindest man who ever lived."

Palfrey said: "How often did he come into this field?"

"He hadn't been here for months; not since sowing."

"I see. Three months?"

"Nearer five."

"What machine was used here then?"

"The plough. That's very heavy, too."

So it was possible that if this city had been here at the time of ploughing, the damage to it would have been done then. It was not a certainty, simply one of the possibilities which passed through

Palfrey's mind; a possibility that rested on the inference that this whole community had built its home here in a few weeks.

"Have you heard any rumours of a plague of rabbits?" he asked.

"No." She was quite definite.

"Any animals?"

"No."

"Have there been many rabbits, this year?"

"Not since they were killed off by myxomatosis."

"These two you saw," said Palfrey. "How big were they?"

"Very big. More the size of hares." Betty looked about her, at the tiny bodies, and then turned towards Palfrey, catching her breath: "You don't think these—" she broke off, as if horrified at the thought that two of these creatures had in fact attacked the stranger, and later killed her husband.

The lieutenant, standing by, came up; a boy turning into a man very quickly.

"Excuse me, sir."

"Yes?" Palfrey asked, absently.

"Shall we search the ruins?"

Palfrey stared at him almost blankly.

"No," he said at last. "Not yet. We ought to have the place checked for—" he hardly knew what for. Gas? Poisons? Living midgets? All he knew for certain was that they must be extremely careful, that men well-versed in detailed searching must be used: rescue squads, yes. Civil Defence workers? Perhaps. All of these working together would get the best results. Mine detectors would be needed too; and what about Geiger counters?

As the thought came to him, he knew that every possible risk must be considered before anything was done. Had he been emphatic enough with his instructions and requests? One of the great dangers of reaching a position like his was the tendency to believe that only he was capable of taking full responsibility. It wasn't simply vanity or arrogance or big-headedness; it was a genuine fear that things would go wrong because no one else knew all he knew. One positive thing was that these ruins must be examined for all possible dangers. The only group competent to do this was a Nato Research Company, and Nato could best be approached through the British Prime Minister.

Time was the big anxiety, for a situation of which they had known practically nothing a few days ago, was now a matter of desperate urgency. There was a code for nearly all emergencies, of course; in these days of fantastically fast aggressive action, with weapons travelling beyond the speed of sound, minutes could matter. Out of his memory came the code number for Nato Research; NR12. He looked at the young officer.

"Does NR12 mean anything to you?"

"I've worked with it, sir."

"Good. Tell your H.Q. I would like NR12 in operation here, before dark. It can't possibly be more urgent."

"I'll fix that at once." The youth was obviously raring to go. "Would it be in order to make a preliminary search, sir? The corporal has been in command of a bomb disposal squad for years, he won't take any chances."

"Call H.Q., and then let's get cracking." Palfrey decided.

There was a risk, of course, of attack and of gas or bacteria undetected by smell, but the dead men had died of blood-letting. No weapons had been used, and he had seen none in the hidden city. He felt that he had earned a few minutes respite, not only for himself but for this woman who needed help and strength to draw on. He did not think there was any reasonable precaution he had forgotten, and so he could give her all his attention. She was walking along the edge of the subsidence sector, rather too close, but trying the earth at every step, obviously aware of the danger. He moved after her, not really able to understand why she was so intent on what she was doing.

Then he saw that she was staring at a tiny hand. It was jutting out of a pile of stubble-littered earth, so tiny that it looked like a doll's. It was limp; no doubt another dead creature was buried there. Palfrey watched as she bent nearer. She poked cautiously at the earth and Palfrey wanted to hurry after her, curious to know why she was so intent.

Then he saw.

The hand did not stick out of the earth, but out of a sleeve, a furry sleeve; and the finger nails were like talons of steel. Heart beating very fast, Palfrey drew still nearer. He did not interfere as Betty scraped the earth away, revealing first an arm, fur-wrapped, then the head and shoulders, then a whole body. There was no possible doubt that Betty Fordham had solved the mystery: the 'rabbits' were these midget men, dressed in rabbit skins.

So they were murderers; deadly killers.

Chapter Six

THE COLONY WHICH DISAPPEARED

Betty Fordham straightened up slowly, still looking at the figure she had revealed. With that trick of not showing any kind of surprise, she spoke without glancing at Palfrey. Her voice was quite calm and unemotional.

"Do you see what I see?"

"Yes. The proof that you were right in saying you saw rabbits attack a man."

"These are the creatures who killed my husband."

Palfrey nodded.

"I want to work with you," Betty said.

"For revenge?"

"In a way."

"Revenge doesn't make for good detection."

"It wouldn't affect my judgement," she asserted.

"I would need proof of that."

She didn't answer, but turned to look at Palfrey and there was almost a touch of humour in her eyes, as if even in the face of tragedy, she could laugh; or at least, see the funny side of a situation. She was a handsome woman, although it was a handsomeness not immediately apparent. Her eyes were greenish-grey in colour, and her skin almost without blemish.

"You are *the* Dr. Palfrey, aren't you? Of Z5?"

So many crises had made it impossible to conceal who he was or what he worked for; Z5 was no longer a secret department, although so many of its operations were unknown to the world.

"Yes," he said.

"I am alone," she stated simply. "Dave was all I lived for. The farm can be sold. I am no good as a farmer, although I got by as a farmer's wife. I'm out of work, and I could be very useful to you."

"What makes you so sure?" asked Palfrey.

"I'm never afraid for long," she said. "Not after the first shock."

"Indeed?"

"Don't laugh at me if I say that there's something in my metabolism which acts like a tranquilliser. Dave used to swear that I was the most even-tempered woman he had ever met, that nothing ruffled me. It doesn't, I promise you. Let me work for you, please."

The appeal was so simple and direct that Palfrey was nearly lured into agreeing. Nearly, but not quite. Instead he smiled gently, and put a hand on her arm.

"If I can, I will."

"Are you the one to decide?"

"Yes," Palfrey said. "I have to, eventually. That's why I can't afford to make any mistakes about the people who work for Z5."

"Meaning that you will screen me."

"Of course. Thoroughly."

"I shall come through satisfactorily," she announced in a matter-of-fact tone. "There's nothing anyone can find out against me. How long will it take?"

"Some days."

"It's an age since David died, already." Betty Fordham said. "Is there anything I can do while I'm on probation?"

She took it for granted that the only thing which stood between her and his trust was time, and he did not believe this was the moment to disabuse her. Nor could he be sure that there was no task for her, even though she was a risk, at this moment. It was surprising that she had not reminded him that a short while ago he had been forced to trust her, and had asked her to help him.

He bent down, and picking up a stone stirred the rabbit man, making sure he did not touch the body with his bare fingers. He called to mind the way she had described the rabbits leaping at Neil Anderson, and he wondered what would happen if a hundred, even a dozen, of such creatures were let loose in a crowd.

He shivered.

"It's horrible, isn't it," Betty said. "Horrible." She looked at him steadily, and went on: "Is this colony the only colony, or are there lots of others?"

Quite truthfully, Palfrey said: "I don't know for certain. I think there is at least one other." He did not add: "In the Congo."

"Then you'd better not lose any time finding out how many," she said, authoritatively, and before he could comment she went on: "Do you think we'll catch all those that were here?"

"I don't think they've a chance of escape," Palfrey said, but even as he answered, he felt the chill of fear, for there was no way of being sure. The certain thing was that he must go back to London and alert the world's governments of the acute danger.

Imagine what could happen if *millions* of creatures like these were in existence. The thought made him shiver inwardly, but outwardly he showed no sign. He turned back to the soldiers, as the corporal appeared, a short man towering above the buildings of the 'city'.

"The place is cleared right up," he said. "They took everything. Couldn't have got far, though, could they?"

"No," answered Palfrey, but in fact he could not be sure.

Others knew and did not really believe it.

Jim Baretta, in a helicopter travelling slowly above and in the wake of the smokescreen knew, but realised that it would be almost impossible to convince Palfrey, or anyone else.

Six helicopters and four conventional reconnaissance aircraft kept a watch on the cloud which might be mist or smoke or gas. The smoke, as all of them called it, was greyish white, and moved sluggishly. It did not appear to thicken, nor to disperse. Thousands of photographs were taken from heights of a hundred to five thousand feet above the ground. Infra-red, and other much more penetrative photographic rays, were used, and most of the photographs were developed instantly. Nothing penetrated the outer layer of the smoke, and nothing at all appeared at the periphery.

Research workers and army decontamination squads moving in the wake of the cloud at ground level, found nothing poisonous or harmful as far as they could judge; there were damp traces and patches of ordinary vapour or mist. The chase went on until dusk fell, and then the cloud stopped moving. Messages were flashed back to Z5 and were relayed to Palfrey who was on his way back to London.

"Smokescreen has been stationary for three minutes."

"Smokescreen has been stationary for five minutes."

"Smokescreen has been stationary for ten minutes."

Ten minutes – fifteen – twenty–

Palfrey stepped out of the helicopter. London's lights were gay and bright over the river and West End, as its millions moved towards the rest and relaxation of evening. A decision would soon have to be made whether to force some penetration of the smokescreen, and Palfrey decided to consult with the Commander-in-Chief of Southern Command before making up his mind. He reached Green Park underground station, stepped into the secret lift, went down, and along to his office. As he passed Joyce's room, she opened the door, and he saw at once that she was distressed.

"Sap."

"What is it?"

"That smoke dispersed."

"Dispersed?" he echoed, and felt the icy clutch of fear.

"Yes," Joyce told him. "And there was nothing beneath it. All of those little creatures had disappeared. Sap – where could they have gone ?"

At this juncture, Palfrey knew, there was no way of telling.

He studied the reports, and the photographs, and was forced to accept the fact that a group of hundreds of pygmies, or midgets, call them what you will, had disappeared without a trace. In the morning, in full daylight, some traces might be found, but by then it would be very late to follow the trail.

Palfrey found his heart beating very fast with a new kind of apprehension. What would the creatures do? Whom else would they attack? What were they? Where had they come from? The obvious thought, which he had forced to the back of his mind, was that they might be from another planet, a possibility which the most sceptical of men accepted today. But while life might have developed on other planets, and something akin to human intelligence might exist, was it likely that physical evolution would be so close to that of the human being of this earth? He did not, could not know; but all reason made him doubt whether it could be so.

If his doubts were justified these must be earthbound creatures. Yet there was something so unreal, so uncanny; even he, used to the bizarre and the terrifying, to phenomena on the borderline of the fantastic and the supernatural, was deeply affected. The worst feature was the utter lack of knowledge, the fact that the first indications had come as matters of interest rather than alarm. Pondering this, he sat down at his desk, and rang for Joyce. She came in at once, a nice girl with a nice figure and a kindly nature.

"Any more reports from overseas?"

"None at all."

"I'll do a special memorandum which must be sent out tonight," said Palfrey. "Can you stay?"

"Of course," Joyce looked almost affronted at the implication that there might be any doubt how late she would work.

"Good. No one can read my writing quite like you." He leaned back and closed his eyes, suddenly very weary. He was aware of her standing and looking at him, and he went on without opening his eyes. "You've seen all the reports, as they've come through, haven't you?"

"Yes."

"What do you make of it?'"

"It's—" she hesitated. "It's terrifying."

"A major emergency."

"Unquestionably."

"Yes," said Palfrey. "I'm going to draft that request for information, and take it over to the Prime Minister. I'd like him to call a meeting of ambassadors, so that the news can be sent to all governments by special courier.

"What worries me most—" he broke off.

"The disappearance," Joyce hazarded.

"No." Palfrey opened his eyes and looked steadily into hers, aware that a question which had been teasing his subconscious for hours, had come to the surface. "We can't be sure how long they were in that field, at the most it was a few months. In that time they built a whole subterranean city, in miniature. Why weren't they noticed before? And how did they learn the engineering methods? What did they model their city on? I'm less worried by their disappearance than in the fact that they were able to imitate us so accurately, and that they could stay unnoticed for so long." He sat up suddenly, his expression changing, his eyes glistening. "These reports of food losses in Southampton, twenty miles from Salisbury. How much food? How many other grain and food warehouses in the area have suffered depredations. We need to find out, quickly. Is Jim Baretta back?"

"No. Galsworthy is in, though."

"Put him onto this," Palfrey said. "Arrange an appointment with the Prime Minister for half past nine or thereabouts. Send me in some sandwiches and coffee, and then forget me until I've finished the draft.

The Rt. Honourable James Mason, M.P., the Prime Minister of the United Kingdom was an energetic and vital man in his middle fifties, comparatively new to his job, alert, anxious to make sure that he missed nothing that mattered. He had been well-briefed about Z5 during his term as Leader of the Opposition, and he knew that Palfrey would not ask for an interview without good cause. Nevertheless, he was host and main speaker at a charity dinner at the Guildhall that night, and would not change his plans. So he arranged to be called from his table at nine-fifteen, and when he met Palfrey in an ante-room, shook hands and said briskly: "I've twenty minutes, Dr. Palfrey. I'm sorry it can be no longer."

Palfrey blinked at him.

"I see, sir." He was so obsessed by what he had learned that he hardly believed that this dark-eyed, alert man could be serious about a time restriction. "The matter may take a little longer."

"It mustn't. I've a major policy speech to make in twenty minutes."

Palfrey felt his annoyance rising, but fought it back. He took a folded sheet of paper from his pocket and handed it to the politician, who unfolded it at once.

"I've sent that to all my offices and agents throughout the world, sir. I would like you to call a meeting of ambassadors – one which I can address – as early as possible. It's better if you convene the meeting as an unusual diplomatic measure – some of the newspapers will catch on if I do it." He stopped, while the Prime Minister read his urgent request to Z5. This said:

Major emergency, Code ZXI. Reason to believe existence of a race of midget men with all human characteristics, apparently living in underground cities, with every modern amenity Stop. These midgets sometimes appear in the guise of rabbits; they might appear as other animals in other places Stop. They are known to attack the throat, puncturing the carotid artery, and by so doing cause death very quickly. They are extremely agile and can leap at least three feet without a running start Stop. They are carnivorous but it is possible they live near cereals ready for harvesting or big grain stores; other food stores may also be vulnerable Stop. A colony which I estimate at five hundred male and female adults and children vanished today after being discovered by accident. They might now be anywhere in Southern England. Reports from Tokyo, the Congo, the United States, China and England indicate they might exist in many parts of the world. The search should be given absolute priority.

The Prime Minister put the paper down staring blankly at Palfrey, giving the impression that he had not taken in the full significance of what he had read. He rubbed his eyes, as if they were tired.

"I see," he said at last. He pressed a bell for the detective who stood outside the door, and the man came in at once. "Inspector, will you give my compliments to the deputy leader and tell him I may be further delayed. If I am not back by ten o'clock he must make my speech for me. He has a copy." He turned to Palfrey. "Is there any danger of this leaking out, Palfrey?"

Expecting opposition, or at best a diplomatic temporising, Palfrey was conscious of tremendous relief.

"Yes, sir. I've instructed the Wiltshire Police to talk about an unknown species of rats which might spread disease."

"Good idea. I'll arrange for an inspired leak about that, then. Ambassadors being ambassadors, I would say twelve noon tomorrow for drinks before luncheon. Will you make sure I receive any reports as they come in—anything you think I should know?"

"I will indeed, sir."

"I'll make a dozen telephone calls, and then try to make that speech on the world food shortage," the Prime Minister added drily. "Food production is falling behind the population growth, year by year. Any threat to staple foods could be deadly in itself. If we've a new form of consumption or wastage—but you know the problem. Good night, Palfrey."

He nodded and moved across to a telephone, Palfrey already dismissed from his mind.

Chapter Seven

THE ALARMING PATHOLOGIST

Palfrey returned to his headquarters in a more relaxed frame of mind than he had known since this affair began. He had learned more about the Prime Minister in ten minutes than in the many hours of previous conversation; here was that truly rare combination, a man of action who could think while he acted. At least there was not likely to be any political obstruction. One factor stood out, moreover; Mason had grasped the implications of the midget men very quickly, and was alarmed.

Palfrey heard no sound as he passed Joyce's door. He looked in. She was lying at full length on a couch, back towards him, obviously tired out. He went to his own room and put the finishing touches to his message, then called for one of the headquarters staff to distribute it. Most agents, even in remote parts of the world, would have it by morning, there might well be a flood of reports by tomorrow evening. He ran through some incoming reports which Joyce had already put on his desk. Only one referred to his earlier note about the ravages of food; a big sugar warehouse in Southern Germany, near Munich, had been practically emptied.

"*Depredation by rats is suspected.*" The report finished.

It was half past ten. Palfrey got up, went to an easy chair, and switched on a radiogram; a hi-fi rendering of a Brahms concerto crept softly into the room, relaxing, comforting. He even began to wonder whether he was worrying too much about these midgets, but suddenly he had a vivid mental picture of Betty Fordham, in the moment when she had realised that her husband was dead. She was quite a remarkable person, and it was easy to believe she meant it when she said that fear did not last long with her. Could Z5 find a use for her services? He made a note: *Screen Betty Fordham,* wrote an instruction about it, then rang for a messenger.

"Put this in hand at once."

"Yes, sir."

Palfrey went back to his chair. His mood had changed, and the face of the woman was constantly in his mind, as well as acute awareness of the way the midget men attacked. He was on edge now, and wanted to talk to the pathologists, but they would still be at their job and it would be pointless to attempt to hurry them. Suddenly it came to him that he had asked Kenneth Campson to carry out an autopsy on Neil Anderson, not on the midget men. What was the matter with him? He rang for Joyce, forgetting for the moment that she had been sleeping, but when she did not come in at once, he remembered.

Very soon, she was at the door, her alert intelligence little impaired by the summary awakening.

"We want autopsies carried out on the 'rabbit' men," he said abruptly.

Joyce stared. "Yes. Of course. I took that for granted. I told Mr. Campson so."

"Oh," said Palfrey. "That's fine." He could have laughed at himself in his deflation; he must never forget how much could safely be left to others. "I've sent off the general request for news – with the Prime Minister's blessing. And I'm having Mrs. Fordham checked. We might find her very useful. You go back and rest – the reports should be coming in soon, and once they do, there won't be much chance of relaxing."

"Sap," Joyce said, after a pause.

"Yes?"

"Don't do too much yourself, please. You look tired out already. You never make allowances for the nervous energy you use up at the beginning of an investigation."

"I'll be careful," he promised, aware that his response was glib and unconvincing.

"May I make a suggestion?"

"Of course."

"Ask Stefan to come to London."

She knew, and Palfrey knew, that Stefan Andromovitch, the second-in-command of Z5, was the only man who could really share the burden of responsibility, one who would think along the same lines, with the same vigour as Palfrey. Stefan was in charge in Moscow and the Far East, because he knew so much more than Palfrey about the mentality, the customs, the traditions and the pride, of Orientals.

"I'll think about it," Palfrey said. "If this affair grows as I'm afraid it will, he'll be needed in Peking as much as I'll need him here."

"I suppose so," she said, her voice troubled.

"I'll lean on you!"

She looked at him steadily, and her lips curled in an un-amused smile.

"I used to think I could give you the kind of help you need, but I've long realised I can't. I began to think Lady Diana Hall could, but she can't either, can she?"

Almost reluctantly, he said. "She lives too much in the future she thinks should be the present."

"And I don't live vividly enough in the world you're trying to improve. Sap – you can't go on alone. You really can't. You need companionship of a kind you simply haven't got. Music, books, the arts, they're not enough. They're really not enough."

She meant what she said deeply, and in one way he agreed with her. He wished he felt differently towards her, but knew he was never likely to. She was still smiling in that impersonal, half-sardonic way, and he had no doubt that there was much on her mind she had not said. She was so good, so right, so determined.

"I get by," he said.

Joyce took a step forward, surprising him by her intensity: "Sap, you don't get by! Every day takes a little more out of you. You're drawing on your reserves far too often. I've known you take a situation like this in your stride but you haven't taken this one in your stride, have you?"

How right she was!

"You need someone to relax with, you need—" Joyce broke off. "Oh, I don't mean you need *sex*! Sap—" She came towards him, hands outstretched, no sign of the sardonic twist to her lips now. "Sap, you're starved of affection. You're the most affectionate man I've ever known, and you've never really had it since your wife died, have you?"

It was impossible even after six years to think of Drusilla, his wife, without hurt.

"No," he admitted, "but you're wrong, Joyce. I can get along very well with my music and my books and my friends."

But when she had gone, he knew that he was lying to her and to himself, and she had forced him to think of Drusilla, whom he had loved so much, who had truly been part of him. He was restless again, disgruntled, even a little resentful that Joyce had done this to him, although he knew that was unfair. He sat back, losing himself in a piano concerto by Liszt ... and did not realise he had dozed.

He heard his name called, and felt a hand on his shoulder. "Sap."

His eyes opened instantly. Joyce was standing in front of him, obviously alarmed. Sleep fell away, and his voice was crisp and sharp.

"What is it?"

"Mr. Campson is here."

Campson. The pathologist.

"But I understood he was at Salisbury."

"He wanted to see you in person."

"Right," said Palfrey. "Where is he?"

"In my office."

"Bring him in," Palfrey said.

She hesitated.

"What is it?" he demanded. "What else is there?"

"We've had the reports from villages around Salisbury," Joyce told him. "At least a dozen shops and warehouses have been broken into, and cereals stolen. Other food has gone, too, particularly sugar and chocolate. And—"

"Yes?"

"Three people have seen the rabbit men."

"Not the midgets?" He thought of the tiny, hairless creatures.

"No. Rabbit men," she insisted, and panic was not far away from her.

Palfrey stood up, very slowly.

"Three you say? Right." He hesitated, almost afraid to go on, but forced himself to ask: "Any more attacks?"

"No. Not yet."

"Is there anything I've overlooked?"

"I don't think so," Joyce replied. "The military and the police had been alerted, all storage places for staple foods are being checked – if any of the 'rabbit' men or the midgets are seen, we'll be told. There's no trace of the smokescreen, and surprisingly little trace of the passage of the colony over the countryside. We can't really do anything more until we've located another colony, can we?"

"Or the Salisbury colony," Palfrey remarked. "We want to examine the area over which the cloud was seen, find out if, or where, they've dug themselves in. The whole area must be minutely scrutinised. All right, send Mr. Campson in."

Kenneth Campson was not only the nation's leading pathologist ... he was an old friend of Palfrey from medical school days, and he had done a great deal for Z5. One thing was quite certain: he would not have come here to report in person unless he felt his evidence was serious enough to be brought to Palfrey's ears alone. He came in, a rather attenuated man with veiled blue eyes, and an air of casual untidiness. In many ways he was not unlike Palfrey, and it would have been easy to take them for brothers. Now, he seemed to be labouring under some strong emotion.

"Hallo, Ken." Palfrey waved a hand in brief salutation. "What will you have to drink?"

"Nothing, thanks – Joyce is going to bring in some coffee."

"Good. Sit down." There was a pause. "What's on your mind?" When Campson did not answer immediately, Palfrey went on: "Neil Anderson?"

"Bled to death," the pathologist said. "But—" he caught his breath.

"Yes?"

"There was something else I haven't yet been able to diagnose," said Campson.

"What sort of thing?"

"A kind of blood condition," the pathologist answered. "Blood samples are being tested. I don't know for sure but I suspect bleeding was much faster than usual, and the blood seemed to thin out, not coagulate, when it first came into contact with the air. I'm very puzzled by it." Campson stretched his legs out, and went on: "I can tell you one other thing."

"Go on."

"The dwarf corpses have the same human blood characteristics as Anderson's. They are very thin-blooded. I've never come across anything quite like it." Palfrey could have echoed: "Nor have I," but he did not. "They are fully mature males as far as I can judge. Average height twelve and a half inches, and the variation is no more than half an inch. The size of arms, legs, heads, necks, chests, waists, hands, and feet hardly vary. They could almost have been turned out of the same plastic mould."

Palfrey didn't speak, touched with a kind of horror which obviously affected the pathologist.

"The weight of each one is practically identical—one pound twelve ounces," Campson went on. "Their muscles are the same size and strength as far as I can judge – their leg muscles in particular are exceptionally well developed. I'm not surprised they can jump several feet from a standing start. I get the impression of absolute physical fitness – the peak of condition. All of those I saw died of suffocation."

Palfrey was listening to this recital in a curious mood, almost of disbelief. His mind was not working as it should do, and he thought of Joyce, and confounded her perception.

"What else?" he demanded.

"There isn't much else – except this almost unbelievable uniformity. All the organs are healthy as far as I can judge – eyes, ears, nails, hair, all are perfectly normal. The bodies don't appear to be subject to the usual human infant variations."

"Brains?" asked Palfrey.

"For their proportions, remarkable in both size and weight."

"Hearts?"

"The same answer." Campson sat upright as the door opened and Joyce came with coffee on a tray. "They're real, Sap. There's nothing synthetic about them. They're real flesh and blood, even if the blood is thin." He smiled in a strained way at Joyce: "Can't you make sure this man gets more sleep, my dear?"

"Now don't you start," said Palfrey. "Pour out for us, Joyce." He went on in the same level tone of voice: "Not synthetic, you say ... Does that mean mammals?"

Campson said jerkily: "Oh, yes. They're mammals all right – the sexual organs are normal except for being so tiny." Campson stretched out for a cup of coffee; his hand was shaking.

"Could they be automatons?" Palfrey demanded.

"Scientists have been trying to create human life for a long time and obviously it's conceivable they'll succeed one day. If they do, then the resulting creatures might not be unlike these midgets. They could be artificially created and incubator bred. I don't say they are, I simply say they might be."

Palfrey took a cup of coffee.

"Yes. We're all guessing. Stomach contents?"

"Mostly carbo-hydrates."

Palfrey moistened his lips: "Teeth?"

"They're probably carnivorous, but haven't eaten much meat lately. One thing isn't quite normal," went on Campson. "Their stomachs are larger, in proportion to the rest of their bodies, than any other organs. I would say they've very healthy appetites, and their food goes to muscle. Usually with a mainly carbo-hydrate diet it runs to fat. There's some factor in their metabolism which might be exactly what we've wanted for the cure of obesity.

However, that isn't quite what you're worried about, is it?" He was more composed now; the telling had eased his mind.

Palfrey said: "Not yet."

"Well don't shout too soon," warned Campson. "There's one factor that worries me a great deal. This blood condition is allied to certain forms of leukaemia. There is a trace of radioactivity in the cells, and the condition is not unlike the early stages of leukaemia caused by exposure to atomic radiation. I don't know the significance of it, but I do know that you should call in your specialists on the effect of atomic radiation on the human body. If these people are radioactive in any way, they might be like disease carriers – always able to pass the disease on to others but inoculated against it themselves. I didn't want to tell anyone else this – I imagine you would like the findings to be a close secret until you really know the strength of them, wouldn't you?"

He didn't add: "And what that strength proves to be is the thing which terrifies me."

Chapter Eight

NO SENSE OF FEAR

Palfrey sat very still and silent. Joyce stirred. Campson, with an assured matter-of-factness, held out his cup for more coffee, and the girl did not notice immediately. Palfrey began to twist strands of hair round his forefinger.

"Radioactivity," he said, almost mumbling. "Nasty thought. Joyce."

"Yes."

"Telephone Harwell, immediately. We would like Professor Copuscenti and his staff to examine these bodies independently of Mr. Campson's report. Ask him to treat it with extreme urgency. Is Baretta back?"

"Yes."

"Tell him to make all arrangements – Harwell's not far from Salisbury, there's no reason why the examination should not be carried out there."

"I'll see to it," said Joyce. She noticed Campson's cup, took it, poured out, and then stretched out for Palfrey's. He waved her away. She went out immediately, while Palfrey continued to toy with those strands of silky hair.

"Cheer up," said Campson, better now that the report was off his mind. "I may be wrong."

"And if you're right, then we know that radioactive midgets are running loose in the Salisbury area, and probably all over Southern

England." Palfrey gave a little bark of laughter. "We've inspired a rumour that we're worried about rats spreading disease."

"That's what I call prescience," said Campson. "What about my written report?"

"One for me, one for the Prime Minister. That will be enough."

"Right," said Campson. He finished his coffee, and stood up, looking down at Palfrey with some seriousness. "You need a rest, old chap. Don't ask too much of yourself, even over this. Spread the load as much as you can."

Palfrey nodded and Campson let himself out, without looking back. Palfrey did not stir from the chair, for a long time, and was still staring at the ceiling, when Joyce returned, carrying a sheaf of papers.

"Professor Copuscenti is on his way to Salisbury," she announced.

"That's good," Palfrey mumbled.

"These reports have just come in," Joyce went on. "There was a delay in the Telstar V system, or we would have had them before." She handed Palfrey the sheaf, and waited as he looked through them.

They came from Buenos Aires, Toronto, Vancouver, Los Angeles, Johannesburg, Hanoi and Budapest. Each one gave details of heavy losses of grain and cereal stocks as well as sugar and chocolate unsuspected until the checking began. The losses were substantial enough in each case to cause local concern; in Hanoi, the losses were great enough to threaten the winter foods for the populations of large areas. With these added to the reports already in, there was enough to give cause for alarm throughout the world. One urgent problem would be to make sure that fear did not spread among the common people, and so produce the seeds of panic.

As the thought entered his head, those very fears began to stir in him, spreading throughout his body. The sense of responsibility bit into him, the duty that his knowledge and awareness of danger imposed on him alone. The common people were, in the main, ignorant of the fact that any radioactive substances should be handled with extreme care, the handlers wearing protective clothing from head to foot even when such material was kept behind thick glass and handled by remote control. If Campson was right, radioactive objects were running loose in many parts of the world. Whether he was right or not, some particularly hideous situation was upon them. 'A certain form of leukaemia' was frighteningly vague. Wastage of the blood cells, wastage of the body – yes, hideous was the word. But radioactivity?

The mist which had hidden the creatures had not been radioactive, or he would have been told.

Palfrey stirred, and thought. "I've touched the bodies. I walked about those ruins."

He did not remind himself in so many words that he could be in deadly danger. So could Betty Fordham. He thought idly and irrelevantly that the name Betty was wrong for her. The thought passed, and awareness of the danger swept over him again.

At half past two, he took a couple of sleeping tablets. By three o'clock he was heavily asleep, and he did not stir until a little before eight o'clock next morning.

After the first moment of waking he recalled the intensity of fear, and half-longed for, half-hated the thought of, the report from Professor Copuscenti. It hadn't come in, and he felt no ill-effects from yesterday's activity; it was probably a false alarm. Apart from the danger of radioactivity there was plenty to worry about. He had a shave and a shower, tea and toast, and sent for Joyce. She looked rested and reassuringly normal; but then she always looked the same.

There were a dozen or so further reports of food losses, of rabbit men having been seen near Winchester, Basingstoke and Warminster, but none appeared to have attacked human beings. All of these places were within easy distance of Salisbury, and might be from the missing colony. There was a request from Mrs. Betty Fordham, she had spoken to those who had seen the rabbit men, and believed she could tell him something he would find very useful.

Joyce said helpfully: "Why don't you see her at breakfast?"

"Where is she?"

"At Brown's Hotel. I suggested she should wait there."

"Good idea," said Palfrey.

The sleeping tablets had not had the refreshing effect of natural sleep. His mood settled into one which made him heavy-headed as well as heavy-hearted. He needed time to think about the situation without having to make decisions – and yet he was almost afraid to think. He certainly needed at least an hour and a half with new reports before he went to the meeting of diplomats, where he would have to weigh every word. My God! What would the effect be if rumour spread that there was radioactivity in the creatures? Even if untrue, it would cause terror. And the truth, whatever it proved to be, might be as bad, or even worse. Panic welled up again and he fought it down. Panic – probably an emotion unknown to a person of the calm capability of Betty Fordham.

Palfrey was walking along Piccadilly on a pleasant, slightly hazy morning, surrounded by Londoners beginning their rush to work before he realised the truth, that in spite of his preoccupation with horror, he was looking forward to seeing the farmer's widow.

He entered the Dover Street foyer of the hotel, and walked through to Albemarle Street, searching for her. Could there have been some mistake? He turned, and started back, then saw her looking at him from a deep armchair. She was half-smiling. He was struck unexpectedly by her handsome looks and calm wholesomeness. As he crossed to her, hand outstretched, she stood up and took it, holding it firmly for a moment.

"Thank you for agreeing to see me," she said.

"I didn't find it very difficult."

Her smile deepened.

"You're very gallant this morning."

He laughed. "Am I?" In fact, he felt relaxed and at ease, and was aware of and puzzled by it. "We've a room upstairs where we can have breakfast and you can tell me what news you have." The room was one always held ready for Z5 for interviews which needed to be near the headquarters, and breakfast would be sent up immediately. He led the way to the lift and then to the second floor. They seemed cut off from the bustle of activity below. He unlocked the door and stood aside for her, and she stepped in – and *screamed.*

Palfrey caught a glimpse of a streak of pale brownish-white fur, of tiny hands, of talons clawing at her throat. Betty Fordham reeled back, with the creature clinging to her neck. Palfrey clenched his fist and struck out, and it loosened its hold. But as it touched the ground it leapt again with uncontrollable fury, a wild cat. Palfrey saw the steel claws scratching at the cloth at Betty's neck. He saw another thing; she had shaken off the terror of the shock and was beating at its head with cool deliberation.

Palfrey jumped forward.

He gripped the creature from behind, hoping to be able to pull it free but as he did so the body seemed to go into convulsions. He could feel the sinews hardening to steel as the little body fought and writhed. At least it could not attack Betty again. She leaned against the door, one hand at her throat, and Palfrey feared to see a gush of blood, but he could only think of the creature twisting and writhing in his hands, so convulsively.

He was uncertain how the struggle would end, weakening visibly, when Betty with one decisive movement thrust her arm forward and brought the side of her hand down sharply on the nape of the creature's neck. It stiffened, and went momentarily still. Palfrey felt a flood of relief and of triumph, but almost at once the body re-vitalised, and wriggled free.

"Look out!" Palfrey cried.

But the catlike 'man' did not attack again. It hit the floor with a light thud, and then turned and streaked along the passage. A porter, turning the corner, kicked against it and fell headlong. The creature reached the head of the stairs and raced down. Almost at once a woman's scream rang out. There was a crash of crockery and a thud of someone falling.

Palfrey did not see the creature rush out into the street but Jim Baretta, waiting for him, saw it clearly. Baretta ran after it, and was in time to see it streaking across Albemarle Street in front of a fast-moving taxi. There was a crunch of sound, another scream – and then blood gushed from the stricken creature, which lay with its mouth open wide, teeth showing, its body smashed.

Baretta rushed forward, taking off his coat, and flung it over the hideous sight. But the rumour began.

"It was a dwarf."

"A child."

"A rat."

"A rabbit."

"A cat."

"A dog."

"A child."

"A dwarf ..."

"Get it to the H.Q. we'll have Campson look at it in the laboratory," Palfrey said gruffly, as he reached Baretta in the street. A dozen motorists had stopped, a hundred people gaped, many of them beginning to find their tongues. "All right, Jim?"

"Yes. What happened?"

"It attacked Betty Fordham."

"Is she hurt?"

Palfrey said: "I don't know." He turned on his heel, leaving Baretta to take charge, his heart dropping sickeningly at the thought of what might have happened to Betty Fordham. He had rushed after the creature and that had been the priority, but he wished it had been possible to help the woman – if she was not already beyond help. How could she have survived those two attacks; how could the flimsy material of her scarf have saved her flesh from those cruel talons? He knew that it could not have done.

No one in the hotel took any notice of him; only a porter appeared to have seen what happened, and he was busy with a taxi and a mountain of luggage. Palfrey went stoically up the stairs, and turned the passage expecting to see Betty crumpled up on the floor, dying, if not already dead.

She was by the open door of the room to which he had taken her, smiling faintly.

"Hallo," she said.

"But—your neck." He felt and sounded breathless.

"I was protected," she told him, brushing aside the tatters of her scarf. Beneath was a wide silver necklet, a piece of costume jewellery heavily inlaid with semi-precious stones. 'You did warn me."

"Ah." He drew his hand across his forehead, and it came away wet. "So I did."

"You didn't take your own advice," Betty said.

"I should have."

"Certainly you should."

"I will in future."

"Yes," Betty said severely. "I hope someone will keep you up to that." She turned into the room. "A waiter brought breakfast and left it on a hotplate. I don't think the coffee's too cold."

Palfrey asked: "What happened to the man who fell over the thing?"

"He thought it was a cat."

"And you let him go on thinking that?"

"It seemed the best thing to do," Betty Fordham said practically.

The words of a song, old and once popular, passed through Palfrey's mind. *Cool, Calm and Collected.* No one could have been cooler, calmer or more composed than this woman, who had not yet asked him what had happened downstairs. He sat down at one side of a table laid for breakfast, and motioned towards the coffee pot. She poured out two cups.

"Sugar?"

"No thanks."

"It steadies the nerves."

"Why would you need to know about that?" asked Palfrey. He sipped the hot coffee, and remembered doing so last night, when Joyce had poured out, and Campson had been so full of alarm, and fear had struck deep. Why did he feel calm now? "So you came prepared."

"Yes," she said simply.

"Weren't you frightened?"

"Only for a moment. It wouldn't stop me going along the passage expecting to see another rabbit man at the corner! It's not a boast, and I don't really feel brave; it's simply that I don't react to fear—or apprehension. I never have. I've always accepted a situation as it is. Just as I've accepted the fact of my husband's death. That hurts, but it doesn't stop me from living."

"No, indeed," said Palfrey. He felt composed enough to take the silver cover off a dish of eggs and bacon, and help first Betty, then himself. They sat at the table, and ate without speaking for a few minutes. No one disturbed them; nothing indicated the danger they had faced only a few minutes before.

Suddenly he said: "I couldn't hold it. It was like trying to hold—a polecat."

"I could tell," said Betty, simply.

"Did you see its claws?"

"Only too well. Did you see that the fur was fastened to the skin at the top of the arms and the back of the legs? That's one of the things I wanted to tell you; I've seen the other women who saw the creatures. They all remember the talons, and the fact that the fur seems to be stuck onto the skin. Is that important?"

"It could be very important," Palfrey said.

"I hoped I might have an opportunity to impress you with my perspicacity. I didn't expect to have a chance to demonstrate how calm I can be in a crisis!" She was almost laughing at herself. "I honestly don't feel any sense of apprehension in advance, and even when I'm scared as I was just now it doesn't last for long. The neck-band proves that I listen to advice, doesn't it?" When Palfrey didn't answer at once, she went on: "I could be very useful to you indeed, surely."

"It wouldn't surprise me," said Palfrey. "And you could be very dangerous, too."

"Dangerous?"

"Yes," Palfrey answered soberly. "The creature attacked you, and proved one thing and gave clear indication of another – that there are two classes, or groups, of these things. Although some of them are certainly very primitive, others have a high intelligence – not only an inventive and technological intelligence, but a reasoning one, too. They followed you and tried to kill you.

The obvious reason which springs to mind is that they were intelligent enough to know you could describe them, and they wanted you dead, so that you couldn't."

Betty Fordham said huskily: "I know what you mean. But now you have seen one, and that puts you in danger."

"Too many have seen them for that to be dangerous much longer," Palfrey reasoned. "They're intelligent enough to realise that—"

"Or some of them are," Betty interpolated.

Palfrey looked at her wryly.

"Or some of them," he agreed. "And apparently they're intelligent enough to appear as rabbits in the country, and cats in town. On the other hand, they're stupid in some ways. Why kill Anderson, for instance – why not just let him walk by?"

Betty hazarded: "Perhaps he had seen and recognised them and the intelligent ones wanted to make sure he couldn't describe them to anyone."

Palfrey looked at her searchingly, but obviously with approval.

"I don't suppose we'll ever know for certain, but that's the most convincing reason I've heard yet. Now let's get back to the point. You could be dangerous to us because you can recognise them – and *they* can recognise you."

"Aren't we all going to be in danger until this menace is over?" Betty demanded. "And aren't you going to need all the help you can get?"

Chapter Nine

A MEETING OF DIPLOMATS

Yes, Palfrey thought, he was going to need all the help he could get, and this woman might be able to help a great deal. Her steady nerve and quite remarkable composure at times of danger made her exactly the stuff of which Z5 agents were made. But he did not trust her yet. As the thought entered his head, he changed it; he could not trust her yet. Circumstances might arise in which he would have to, but until they did he would need to be very wary. Even if she passed the intensive screening which had already been put in hand, he might trust only after a period of trial. Yet the clarity of her blue eyes, the frankness of her manner, the wholesomeness which was so evident, made him want to trust her now. He recalled the French expression: "Good as bread". It suited her perfectly.

Quietly, she asked : "You don't trust me, do you?"

"Not in the way I would have to," Palfrey said.

"You've simply forgotten how to trust," she accused.

There was a great deal of truth in that.

"I dare not trust anyone easily," Palfrey said. "Experience has taught me that practically no one is wholly trustworthy."

"I didn't think you would be cynical."

"Is that being cynical?"

"You've virtually said that everyone has his price."

"And everyone has," Palfrey declared. "No, don't resent that. Everyone has, but I don't mean everyone can be bribed, that's

66

taking 'price' too literally. Everyone has a breaking point. And everyone has secret hopes and fears. Some people honestly believe it would be better to live in a Communist or a Fascist world than not to live at all. What about you?"

"I'd rather live," Betty Fordham said.

"So the price you would pay might be to submit to Communist or Fascist pressure," said Palfrey. "I can't take that risk."

"Are you seriously saying this horrible threat is Communist or Fascist inspired?" She looked sceptical, almost angry.

"I'm seriously saying that it might be. I don't know enough yet, to do anything but keep an open mind. This could be some kind of natural phenomenon, without any human cause or control. Or it might be that these creatures are man-made. They might possibly be self-controlled, but conceivably activated by remote control. It's even conceivable that one man has discovered the secret of producing them artificially, and that they've multiplied beyond anything he dreamed. Or one man, a group of men, even a nation, might be using them as a weapon against the rest of the world." Palfrey paused, smiled diffidently, and spread his hands, in a self-deprecatory little gesture. "You see how confused I am."

She was looking at him in a different way now, as if a new respect for him had been born in her.

"I see why you can't trust me."

"Why can't I?"

"I might be involved. My husband might have known the creatures were in the field, and they might have got out of *his* control. They might have followed me because I can tell you much more about them than they want you to know. So you have to doubt me."

"So I do," Palfrey smiled almost angelically, and said the thing which came into his mind spontaneously. "But trusting and liking aren't the same thing. I've enjoyed this breakfast talk more than I have enjoyed anything for many weeks, yet at a time when I'm gravely worried. It's done me more good than I can say." He held out both his hands, and she placed hers on them. "Thank you."

"Dr. Palfrey," she said, not letting his hands go.

"Yes?"

"You *can* trust me. I know that in your responsible position you can't as yet, but in fact I am really absolutely trustworthy."

"I believe you are," Palfrey said. They stood studying each other for a long time, until he thought he would never forget a line or feature of her face. "Now – I must go! Will you stay here until you hear from us?"

"Will I hear?"

"Yes. We'll certainly need to question you again. There may be some details you've forgotten and which we can help you to remember. You'd be surprised what expert questioning can make you recall! And there are some elementary facts about Z5 which you can learn while you're on – what shall I say? – probation."

Her eyes lit up.

"Am I on probation?"

"In principle, I hope very much that you will soon be working for us," said Palfrey.

Betty Fordham began to smile, and the corners of her lips curved upwards, revealing two dimples. They gave her a young, almost mischievous appearance. Good as bread, Palfrey thought again, but even though all his inclination was to trust her, the warning note was clear and vivid in his mind.

"I'll be at Brown's until I'm sent for," she said. "There's one thing."

"Yes?"

"What shall I say if I'm questioned by reporters? Someone might know the little brute came at me, or connect me with it somehow."

Palfrey eyed her quizzically: "Use your own judgement," he advised. "If you join Z5 you'll have to."

"And this is as good a way as any of finding out whether I can be discreet." She actually laughed. "I'll be interested to find out, too."

Palfrey said quickly. "I'm sure you will. Meanwhile don't worry about being followed. I shall have you watched for your own safety."

As he walked slowly to the head of the stairs, he watched the floor and doorways, subconsciously on the look-out, but consciously thinking of Betty Fordham. What was Betty short for? Elizabeth? Beth would suit her better than Betty. He preferred it. Beth was comforting, and that she most certainly was. He was aware that his feeling of relaxation was largely due to her. In a way she had drawn not only tensions out of him, but also something of the sense of urgency. Was that a good or a bad thing? He went into Green Park station and was halfway towards the door leading to his lift when he saw a tiny, furry animal streaking towards him.

Fear burned his chest, with a sudden furious heat.

Then he saw it was a dog, which raced along to the stairs and up them, a black lead trailing. Poor frightened creature. Poor, frightened Palfrey! He actually laughed aloud as he turned into the lift, and his step was lighter as he went along the passage and opened Joyce's door.

"Anything new in?" he demanded.

She stared at him, as if surprised.

"Is there?"

"Er—some more reports," she said, recovering. She stood up, and almost immediately became her normal self, pleasant, precise. "Yes, I'm afraid so. Another four reports have come in that rabbit men have been seen singly in Staines, Guildford, Dorking and Andover." She looked at him, puzzled because he showed no reaction. "Reports from overseas are coming in so fast we can hardly keep up with the decoding," she added. "Some reports are of cats – but the claws all seem to be the same."

"In all future messages, say that the creatures might be in the guise of any small animal which would be familiar in the district it was seen in." Palfrey pondered, and then asked: "Are there more food losses?"

"Yes – as far apart as Stockholm and Sydney, San Paulo and Port Said. I've put an analysis on your desk for the ambassadors' meeting." After a pause, Joyce went on: "The Prime Minister would like you to be at the Foreign Office Assembly Room at eleven forty-five, with up-to-the-minute information."

"I'll be there," Palfrey promised.

"Are you—all right?"

"Yes, of course.'"

"The creature didn't hurt you?"

"No," Palfrey answered. "But all of us who might be attacked ought to be protected. We need some kind of neckband." He thought of the silver one which Betty 'Beth' Fordham had worn. "I wonder who I ought to talk to about that?"

"Weapon Research?" hazarded Joyce.

The Weapon Research Department was a branch of the laboratory domiciled on the floor below. Agents involved in the deadly business were necessarily those possessing ingenious and inventive minds, for the department both created weapons and devised protective steps needed against them.

"Yes," said Palfrey. "Will you tell them exactly what we want? A necklet that will resist a knife thrust, not be too hot or tight, and can be slipped on and off easily."

"There are ordinary bracelets like that," Joyce said. "I'll see to it right away."

"Good," said Palfrey. "Now I'll go and soak myself in the reports."

He found nearly fifty of them on his desk, and read each one with a detachment he had not felt for a long time. He absorbed them, too. Everything he read had some deep significance and increased the gravity of their problem, but he did not feel so utterly hopeless and dejected as he had; he was on top of himself, in spite of the horror. Yet he hadn't been until he had seen Beth. Not Betty; Beth.

The Prime Minister studied a summary of the reports, looked down his nose, and said: "I'll simply set the tone of the meeting, Palfrey. You put the facts to them as directly as you can."

Palfrey said: "I'll do just that, sir."

The Assembly Room, often used for great State occasions, had a high, beautifully decorated ceiling, drapes of grey and silver, and three huge chandeliers. One long table was laden with a selection of cold meats, fish, salads, fruit, cream and wines. Behind this stood Secret Service and Intelligence men and women who would be briefed by Palfrey. There were ten Z5 agents among them, seven men and three women.

As Palfrey followed the Rt. Honourable James Mason into the great room, there was a lull in the buzz of conversation. Palfrey, walking down a flight of wide stairs, fully aware of the fact that the Prime Minister attracted all the attention, and that very few of the assembled diplomats noticed him. He himself recognised dozens, as he took them in with a few sweeping glances. The ambassadors of France, Western Germany, the United States and Japan were in a group together. The Russian, Yugoslavian and Polish ambassadors stood with two from newly emergent African countries, one from Kenya, the other not known to Palfrey. Among the gathering thirty at least were black or dark-skinned. There were three women, engulfed by the horde of well-dressed men. Several African and Arab leaders lent magnificence to the gathering by the vivid colour of their voluminous robes.

Slowly silence fell.

Palfrey and Mason climbed onto a small platform, behind which was a white screen; and as they did so a Z5 man moved into the room, with a slide projector, and another put a table into place for it.

"Your excellencies," the Prime Minister said in a clear, carrying voice, "I have little to say myself, except to prepare you for what may well be a very grave and serious situation. It has sufficient urgency for me to feel that the best way to advise your governments is through the Assembly. In this way, each one of you will know exactly as much as all the others know, each will be able to inform his government at the same time." He paused, timing the moment admirably, looking round at faces which had suddenly become anxious, from which both frowns and good humour had faded. A sea of gravely expectant faces were below Palfrey, and he noticed several of them turned towards him. The Brazilian ambassador, Carlos, deftly nudged the Portuguese ambassador, who immediately looked at Palfrey. So did the handsome Clemente Taza of Lozania.

"I heard of this emergency only fifteen hours ago," the Prime Minister went on, "and I believe that Dr. Palfrey, whom you all know, had no reason to suspect the seriousness of the situation until a few hours before he asked me to convene this meeting."

In some parts of the room, the name 'Palfrey' caused an uneasy consternation. Practically everyone looked towards him, as the clear, precise voice went on.

"It is vital that no rumour of the true reason for this meeting is released to the Press, and following my statement of British Policy on World Food Shortages last night, I believe we should allow it to be thought that this meeting concerns that shortage. As in a way it does." The Prime Minister turned to Palfrey, and went on: "Here is Dr. Palfrey, who needs no introduction to any of us."

As Palfrey stepped forward, the silence was absolute.

He talked for fifteen minutes, feeling quite sure as he did so that he had never put a situation more lucidly nor more comprehensively; at least that was a cause for satisfaction. When he finished, the hush was as great as it had been when he had started, until the Italian ambassador, tall, dark-haired, elegantly bearded, spoke in a high-pitched voice: "If these creatures are so widespread, on several continents, then no country is safe from them. Do you know what they are doing? Why they are here?"

"All we know is that they eat ravenously," Palfrey said. "There is no indication that they have taken any course of action except in order to get food—and to protect themselves. They appear to be at varying stages of intellectual development. You will know from what I have told you that some have highly developed intelligence, while others seem to be primitive. They have many human characteristics."

"What *are* they like?" demanded Taza, the ambassador for Lozania, the smallest South American state.

Palfrey said: "Let me show you." He stood aside, and the man at the projector switched off the lights, and switched on the machine. Pictures of the dead creatures found on Fordham's farm flashed vividly onto the screen in colour.

As the company watched, there was a strange, almost awestruck silence.

There were twelve pictures in all, and each was left on the screen for half-a-minute. Then they were taken away, as Palfrey went on: "Copies of these are being made as quickly as possible and will be available by tomorrow morning. You've noticed the marked difference between the fur-clad creatures, and those which are like midgets. As far as we can judge the furry ones are guards, or killers; and they seem to have a highly developed intelligence, although they appear to act stupidly from time to time.

"How do you mean – stupidly?" asked Conlon, the American ambassador.

"They don't attempt to conceal themselves, but make an attack and rely on their physical strength to get away." When no one commented, Palfrey went on: "We know some appear as rabbits, at least one as cat, so they might adopt other disguises to make themselves less noticeable."

"They've a hell of a lot of courage," Conlon said. "Palfrey, what is your assessment of the danger?"

Palfrey answered briskly: "Ten of these creatures in this room could probably kill us all. If the colony found near Salisbury is the only one in England we might be able to find and contain it, but, if there are others, food stocks throughout Britain will soon be in danger, and so will any people who attempt to protect them."

"This is absurd. They must be found and exterminated." The voice was that of Hertz, the South African ambassador.

"Where are they from?" Halik of Russia asked in his heavily-accented English.

"*Are* they human?" another demanded.

"*Could* they come from another planet?"

"Now, that's crazy!"

"It is understandably alarming," said the ambassador from Lozania. "But is there no hope that this has been grossly exaggerated?"

"Palfrey would hardly exaggerate," Conlon objected.

"Gentlemen!" called the British Prime Minister sharply. "Each of you has been informed, each must report to his government as he thinks fit. We in Great Britain consider this to be potentially a very grave emergency, and arrangements are already in hand for the armed forces to help protect existing food supplies and crops. Dr. Palfrey will keep us all informed of new developments, and I shall continue to give him all facilities. Now, if you care to lunch—" In a few moments he was in the centre of a group of anxious, excited ambassadors, Palfrey in the midst of another. He saw the ambassador from Lozania looking at him with obvious anxiety, and saw several other ambassadors join Clemente Taza. Then he had a sudden, devastating shock. Taza was an unusually good-looking man, with regular features, smooth skin, and controlled grace of movements; Lozanians being renowned for their good looks, and that undefinable quality which marked them as a race apart.

It came to him now that Clemente Taza's features were quite unmistakably like those of the creatures he had seen. It was in the bone structure of the face, the set of the eyes, the shape of the mouth. The similarity could not be mistaken once it had been noticed.

The best man to work on Taza was Jim Baretta, Palfrey decided. He could not get to a telephone quickly enough.

Chapter Ten

THE ANXIOUS AMBASSADOR

Clemente Taza, one of the most efficient and successful career diplomats in South America and an outstanding representative of his own country toyed with a small sliver of *pâté de foie gras,* then hurried from the Assembly Room. His chauffeur was waiting for him, and he was driven off immediately. The Lozanian Embassy was in Prince's Gate, and the traffic through Hyde Park Corner and Knightsbridge was very dense that lunch hour. By the time Taza reached the fine old Georgian house, Jim Baretta was already sitting, double-parked, in a Mini-Cooper which did not earn a second glance. Two more Z5 agents were also watching the house; and others would come. Until Taza had been completely cleared of suspicion, he would be watched day and night. Every move he made, even his telephone calls, would be reported. Inside the Embassy were two Lozanians, each fiercely loyal to *Z5;* Baretta would be in constant touch with them.

Taza went inside. *"Tense and worried,"* Baretta later reported.

Taza went straight to the first secretary.

"They were together for an hour," one of the Z5 agents reported. *"A tape recording will be sent as soon as practicable. I do not know yet what subject was under discussion."*

The first secretary left the house in Prince's Gate immediately after his long talk with Taza.

"He went direct to London Airport," one of Z5's agents reported.

An hour later, another report from inside the Embassy reached Palfrey, who was now back at his office.

"The first secretary was on board the eight o'clock flight to New York."

Within an hour, another message reached Palfrey from the Lozanian Consulate in New York City.

"Two seats have been booked on tomorrow's early flight from Kennedy Airport to Lozan."

Lozan was the capital of Lozania.

"No other member of the Embassy staff appears to be aware of the reason for the first secretary's journey," stated another report. *"The ambassador is now conducting normal daily business. He is obviously preoccupied."*

Palfrey studied these, and many other reports, during the late afternoon, feeling a new weight of anxiety and depression. He kept his mind as unprejudiced as he could, but the possibility of early results made him hope that the secret of the rabbit men and the midgets might be found before too much damage was done. In the early evening he was standing and studying the spines of some of the leather bound books in his study, when Joyce telephoned. He snatched up the receiver.

"Yes?"

"The tape from the Lozanian Embassy is on the way. Baretta is bringing it."

"Thank God for that," Palfrey said. "It's almost certain that Lozania's involved."

"How can you be so sure?" demanded Joyce.

"No other message has gone to Lozan today. It is the only Embassy which has not sent coded messages back to the government at home."

"I see what you mean," Joyce said. "Do you want to take extra copies of the tape?"

"Yes" said Palfrey. "And I would like you, Galsworthy and Bonifacio to be present." Bonifacio could make a simultaneous translation into English, both for his, Palfrey's benefit and for the recordings which might be essential. He waited for the tape to reach Z5 headquarters with almost feverish anxiety. Baretta was one of the best agents, he would have a man in front and two behind him for protection, each wearing a plastic strip round his throat. There was every reason to believe they were strongly safeguarded.

Certainly Jim Baretta was not worried. This short powerful Italian had steel bracelets round his wrists and neck, aware that he might have to fight off one of the creatures.

Outside the Lozanian Embassy he noticed as did the men watching him, a small post office van pulled up near the house as the driver walked to a pillar box, opened it, and took out letters. None of the Z5 men gave this man any further thought. The agent who had planted the tape came out and placed it quite casually on the wing of a car parked nearby. Baretta strolled along and picked it up, slipped it into his pocket and got into the green/white Mini-Cooper. One agent in front was on a motor-cycle, two behind were in an open T.R.3, vivid scarlet; there were times when the best way to hide was to draw attention to oneself.

The little cavalcade moved off.

When Baretta stopped, opposite Green Park underground station, a post office van drew up, not far behind. Its driver got out, and opened the back doors.

A furry streak leapt past him; a second, a third, a fourth.

Two men and a girl, almost level with the van, gaped as the four cat-like creatures leapt past the van towards Baretta. He heard a scream and a honking on the horn of the T.R.3. He swung round, hands up to protect his face, but four of the creatures leapt at him at once, and as he felt their impact, others raced from the post office van. The motor-cyclist jumped off his machine and ran forward – and four of the creatures hurtled at him. He went crashing down. As the other two men jumped up from the T.R.3, four more of the rabbit men sprang at them.

By now, a medley of people were rushing to help, women were screaming, men shouting, a woman cried *"Police, police!"* Huge red buses groaned to a stop, tyres screeched, cars and taxis slithered or jolted to a standstill, a cyclist fell so heavily that he lay stunned.

And more of the creatures came.

They snarled as they leapt at hands and bodies, eyes and faces, until in front of the horrified gaze of hundreds of people, human beings were torn to shreds, mangled, ripped, left unrecognisable. Two policemen, truncheons drawn, rushed up to try to save Baretta, but each was attacked savagely, each felt talons sink into his throat, each fell, dying. A small boy, terrified, turned and ran, slipped – and was suddenly buried by the seething fury of the creatures who looked like cats.

Now, police whistles were screeching, men from buses, cars and taxis recognised the danger, mobile police and the more responsible civilians began to draw the crowd away. One man arranged for a barrier of cars across Piccadilly in one direction, three buses were turned round in the other, to keep the crowd back. Traffic from Hyde Park Corner and from the Mall and St. James's, was held up in a jam thick and solid and unmoving. Emergency calls were made for more police, and for firemen, and others went out for troops.

Near the Mini-Cooper, the T.R.3. and the motor-cycle, were the remains of four of Palfrey's men.

Others, watching, hurried to report to Palfrey.

The Czechoslovakian ambassador to the Court of Queen Elizabeth who had been briefed by Palfrey and was having dinner at a penthouse overlooking Green Park, and very near the scene, heard the commotion and looked out. He saw the crowds gathered near the park railings pressing close, deckchairs and park seats neglected. Then he saw what looked like cats leaping over the railings and among the crowd, the sudden, awful panic. Women and girls in light summer dresses went down beneath a terrible onslaught, throats and faces crimsoned with blood. Two children ran, screaming. The whole park close to the railings was a seething mass of panic-stricken people, running, stumbling, crawling away from the ferocious creatures with the soft, cat-like fur.

The ambassador's colour drained away, and he turned for a telephone.

Newspaper reporters saw what happened and besieged the kiosks and the telephones of shops and offices. Two tourists with eight millimetre cine cameras stood fast, keeping their finger on the trigger, shooting the dreadful scenes. And on a corner of Dover Street, Betty Fordham stood, unmoving, showing no expression.

Among the crowds in the traffic jams were no less than five ambassadors, and of those five none now could doubt what Palfrey had said.

The news of disaster reached Palfrey within ten minutes of it starting. He was out of his office and going towards the lift when Joyce ran after him, pleading "Don't go, Sap, don't take chances." He ignored her. There was danger, always danger, and one could protect oneself too much. Other agents joined him as he hurried towards the shambles, and when he saw the extent of it he was appalled.

He saw Mrs Fordham – and thought of her as Beth.

Somehow, it seemed natural that she should be there; not until afterwards did he wonder at the coincidence. She was very pale. As they walked together towards the scene, he noticed for the first time how tall she was; almost as tall as he. For a moment their hands touched.

"Wait here," Palfrey said.

He pushed his way through the crowd towards the spot where the Mini-Cooper stood, splashed with Baretta's blood. None of the animals was in sight now, except one which had been run over by a bus. Palfrey made himself walk forward, and go through Baretta's pockets, clenching his teeth, fighting back nausea. There was nothing there. He found the tape near the kerb, out of its box, damaged beyond repair, and he knew it would serve no useful purpose. More. He knew that it had been taken out of that packet by one of the creatures, who seemed to have human intelligence, knowing exactly what it wanted and how to get it. He turned back to the pavement and to Betty, whose eyes were level with his above the heads of the crowd. She did not look away. A superintendent of police, who knew him, came up and asked: "Anything we can do for you, Dr. Palfrey?"

"No thanks."

"Can we get the traffic moving yet?"

"I don't see why not."

"Have to wash the road down," the Superintendent said. "I've never seen anything like it. It's worse than a battlefield."

Palfrey muttered: "Yes." It was worse, because so many women and children, boys and girls, had been dreadfully injured, or had died. Worse, because everyone had been so defenceless. Worse, because there had been no warning, and because the savage fury of the killer creatures had been released so swiftly. And in a way, worse because if he had broadcast word of the danger, some of these people might have been prepared – and protected.

At heart, he did not believe this. The world must know now, but at least a little time had been given to governments, to prepare their people, and there was less danger of panic. He could not understand why the attack had been made – possibly to get the tape, possibly – and this he feared most – the creatures, once angered, could not control their savagery. It was as if they had a natural bloodlust.

He put this out of his mind, and reached Betty, thinking: "Why is she here?"

He forced a smile.

"I can't stop," he said.

He went on, with men surrounding him and carrying the tiny tape, the useless tape. He knew that the next thing he must do was see Clemente Taza, but even as the realisation passed through his mind he wondered whether the ambassador was still in England.

He had to find out soon. But first he had to send further warnings out, had to make quite sure that no one underestimated the danger, even though he himself could not yet assess it fully. Back at the office he did all that he had to, and before leaving for the Lozanian Embassy, called in an agent named Armitage. Armitage was a very able agent, almost devoid of imagination, with complete command of several languages, and remarkable resource in emergency. The essence of Armitage's quality was his single-mindedness, and his freedom from emotion. Palfrey had never known him influenced in any way by a woman no matter how beautiful, nor how helpless, and he had never known him influenced by any human situation. He did not believe there was anyone in the world more detached; nor did he believe that anything or anyone could ever corrupt that man, or his coldly intellectual conviction that the world must one day be governed by a World Force. He was a normal enough man in social attitudes, and only those who knew him well realised there was passion behind his intellectual detachment. No one knew why he was known as Tig.

"Tig," Palfrey said. "I want you personally to check on a Mrs. Betty Fordham very closely. Find out what we've already discovered about her, and then have her watched and followed wherever she goes."

"Right," said Armitage.

"Let me hear from you two or three times each day."

"Right."

"Thanks," said Palfrey.

In a strange way, he felt a sense almost of betrayal, but that was nonsense. He would have anyone watched if there were the slightest grounds for suspicion. It was illogical to feel that Betty, or Beth, Fordham should be treated otherwise.

When he reached Piccadilly again, firemen were sluicing down the road with their hoses at half-pressure, but no traffic was yet moving. Large reinforcements of police had been brought up, and were controlling the crowd. There was no possible doubt that this story, with pictures, would reach the early evening papers and television, and it had come too swiftly for him to influence the manner of it. As he stepped into a car with armour-plated sides and bullet-proof windows, he wondered whether he should have telephoned the Prime Minister. Sometimes it was difficult even for him to realise that he owed allegiance to the world first, and to his own country second. There was a radio in the car and he could call Number 10 from here, but he decided not to.

Soon, he was being admitted to the front hall of the Lozanian Embassy, in a quiet, pleasant street in London which seemed far removed from horror. He had been told that Clemente Taza had not left the Embassy, but would hardly have been surprised had he been told that his Excellency was out.

Instead, within two minutes the second secretary was saying: "His Excellency will see you, sir."

The ambassador was in the front room on the first floor. On a closer inspection, Palfrey saw that the amazing good looks and regularity of features that had so startled him held a curious lifelessness. That was particularly odd in a Latin, Palfrey reflected. The handclasp, however, was firm, the greeting most disarming, especially as it was accompanied by a charming smile.

"I owe you an apology, Dr. Palfrey. I was quite wrong to doubt what you told us this morning. Please sit down."

"So you've heard what happened in Piccadilly and Green Park." Palfrey said.

"I have, and may I say that I am greatly shocked."

"Do you know why it happened, your Excellency?"

"No, I do not."

"Then I will tell you. It happened because one of my agents brought a tape recording of a conversation you had with your first secretary, away from here. It was being brought to me. Those creatures I warned you about destroyed it, incidentally causing the death of at least thirty people and grave injury to many more."

Taza said, very quietly, "You cannot expect me to believe that."

"I know it to be true, sir. The man who smuggled the tape out of the Embassy is alive. He is prepared to swear to everything he knows. We can establish beyond any doubt that the trouble started here. It will save us a great deal of time and a lot of unpleasantness if you will accept the situation and tell me all you can."

"And if I refuse to accept the situation?" demanded Taza.

"I would be extremely sorry," Palfrey said, "but I would use my influence to have all your diplomatic privileges withdrawn. And I would use all the resources of Z5 to make you tell the truth. I do not believe you would be able to resist the pressure which would be brought to bear." As the other's colour faded and his lips tightened in anger, Palfrey went on. "And at the same time I would inform all governments that I could prove Lozania's association with the emergency, so that very great pressure indeed would be exerted on your government. I don't think it could be resisted."

"This is blackmail," Taza said hoarsely.

"I hope you understand this, your Excellency," said Palfrey in a hard, unemotional voice. "There is nothing in this world I will not do to make you talk. It is not simply that some of my friends have been torn to pieces, alive, by these demoniac creatures. I have reason to believe they could cause terrible sickness to mankind, as well as ultimate starvation. Neither you nor anyone else who helps to conceal the creatures will get any mercy at all from me or from those who work for me."

Chapter Eleven

THE AMBASSADOR'S REQUEST

Taza did not respond, did not look away from Palfrey. It was difficult to define or understand the expression in his fine, bold eyes. Hatred? Palfrey did not think so. Rage? It was anger, but controlled. Fear? In a way, perhaps that was it. Two spots of colour now burned on his cheeks, as the silence dragged on and on.

At last, he drew a deep breath and said: "You make yourself very clear, Dr. Palfrey. However, you understand that I have instructions, and I must obey them."

"I understand," Palfrey said, quietly, "but it will take longer to learn the truth, and the danger will be greater because of it. Have you really calculated the danger?"

Taza said in the same tense voice: "At best, I can consult my government."

"By telephone?"

"Yes."

"What will you do? Ask their permission to tell us the truth?"

"Yes."

"Will you telephone at once?"

"If you will leave me here," Taza said, "I will speak to His Highness the President as soon as the call comes through."

Would he? wondered Palfrey. Or was he simply playing for time. When Palfrey had left this room, would he go out of another door and flee the country? Would he even kill himself? These risks were obvious, but so were the advantages. Whatever course he took, Taza would virtually make an admission for the world to see. As a fugitive or a suicide, he would be admitting his country's complicity, and so ensure a swift and searching enquiry. It was practically certain that he would in fact talk to his government. Palfrey was on the point of saying he would wait, when a telephone bell rang. Taza, glad of release from tension, picked up the instrument.

"Yes? ... Yes, he is here ... One moment." He held the receiver close to his chest. "It is an urgent call for you, Dr. Palfrey."

Palfrey smiled very faintly.

"Let me take that, while you make your call."

Taza handed him the telephone, gave a stiff little bow, and went out. Palfrey watched the door swing to, and wondered whether anyone was listening outside it, whether there were microphones concealed in this room, perhaps in the telephone itself. At last, he said: "This is Palfrey."

"Sap, Professor Copuscenti and Dr. Walsh are here and want to see you urgently." It was Joyce. "The Professor is very agitated – in fact he's frightened. How soon can you be here?"

Swift as light, Palfrey thought: "Copuscenti is frightened." The Professor was one of the world's leading specialists in the field of the effect of atomic radiation on the human body, on blood cells, on hereditary influences. Palfrey, who understood so much more than the man in the street, could never follow the complexities of Copuscenti's mind, of his research, or of the subject. He did know that no one else in the world had a greater grasp of that subject, that his voice had long been raised, sometimes strident and alone, sometimes as the leader of a frightened chorus prophesying the effect of atomic radiation on the future of the human species.

Now this great physicist had seen the body of one of the little creatures and was frightened.

"Sap," Joyce said. "Are you there?"

"I'll be back within the hour," Palfrey said. "Is—anything else in?"

"The newspapers and television are going mad,' Joyce told him. "The Prime Minister has been trying to get you for the past half hour and wants you to call him at once. And ..." Joyce hesitated, as if even her dispassionate mind was almost overcome by the horror and the magnitude of this situation. "And," she repeated, "more and more reports are coming in from overseas, about serious food losses. In Cambodia, they are down to a month's supply of rice, in Ireland supplies of flour and potatoes are already dangerously low. God knows how long this had been going on."

Palfrey thought: *Taza might.*

"Hold the fort," he said. "I won't be long."

"You mustn't be," Joyce said. Her voice was nearly despairing.

Palfrey rang off, a picture of Copuscenti in his mind. The physicist was a short man with a big head, a leonine head; a popular image of a prophet spoiled by his stubby legs; but for his fine torso and broad shoulders he would have been a dwarf. Palfrey shivered. He seemed to see Copuscenti's fine eyes, to hear his dry impersonal voice with its ironic undertones. "All I am being asked to do, Dr. Palfrey, is to preside over the destruction of mankind so as to make it painless for the individual." Dr. Walsh, whom Palfrey had met only once, was the Professor's colleague and an expert on toxicology and immunology.

Was there a clue in his presence?

The door opened, startling Palfrey. He swung round, to see Taza coming in; it was difficult to imagine a man who looked more different from Copuscenti.

"Dr. Palfrey, I have a most important request to make," he said without preamble.

The mental image of Professor Copuscenti faded.

"Yes?"

"Will you fly to Lozania to discuss this matter with President Mortini? I have spoken to him, and the request is from him. You will of course be guaranteed safe conduct. You will have nothing to fear."

Nothing to fear, echoed Palfrey bitterly.

He said: "Will President Mortini be able to help in this emergency?"

"He will acquaint you with certain facts."

"Will he understand that I will have to have others with me?"

"That will of course be for you to decide."

Palfrey played with his hair, twisting strands round and round. It would take ten hours to fly to Lozania, and a special plane could be made ready in two hours or less – a military jet was always at his disposal. He could take two or three people with him. If Baretta were alive – he gritted his teeth. He would need an interpreter, and someone with a basic understanding of the problem. He thought: Copuscenti knows Portuguese.

"Thank the President and tell him I hope to leave London before midnight."

"He will be very glad," Taza said, and as Palfrey moved towards the door, he added, "Dr. Palfrey, what happened at the Embassy today was without my knowledge. I am sorry."

So he admitted having some control over the cat men.

There was so much to do, quickly. Arrange the aircraft, decide who was to fly with him to Lozan; have the Lozanian Embassy cordoned off and all of its visitors screened, the staff watched and followed; leave instructions for other embassies to be closely watched too. Leave instructions for summaries of the reports to be sent to him ...

And there was Professor Copuscenti to see.

The Professor was afraid.

This man with the noble face, the near-Socratic calm and objectivity, this man whose intellectual brilliance was laced with ironic wit which so often earned him disrepute, this man who could conceive of the destruction of the human race with a Jove-like detachment, was nervous and afraid. His hand was warm and moist; his lips were twitching. It was almost as if he were suffering from the effects of a stroke. He was with Walsh in a small room with lead walls, off the main laboratory at Z5's headquarters. Never still, he moved from chair to chair, and desk to chair incessantly, while Walsh, a small, compact man with a clipped moustache and pointed beard, sat near, still hardly blinking.

"I've told no one yet," he stated. "No one. But these creatures—my God, how does one understand? How does one talk of the impossible. Come." He marched out of the room towards a bench where what was left of one of the creatures was lying. It was inside a glass container of a kind Palfrey recognised; it gave him his first shock, although Copuscenti's manner should have warned him. Atomic reactors were customarily kept inside such boxes. Over by the wall were other boxes, containing the shapeless remains of ordinary men; and of the 'rabbit' and 'cat' men.

Copuscenti handed Palfrey a pair of thick rubber gloves. As Palfrey drew them on, the other put a pair of lead-coated manipulators in his hand. In their jaws was a tiny Geiger counter. None of this was new to Palfrey but never had he felt so appalled as he did now.

"Go on." Copuscenti ordered raspingly.

Palfrey began to manipulate the Geiger counter, and, as it hovered above the mangled flesh and blood, a cracking sound came so sharply and suddenly that although he had expected it, Palfrey drew back.

"You see," Copuscenti muttered. "The blood is radioactive to a degree I have seldom known except in reactors themselves. I have examined men and women who have been subjected to radiation during a nuclear explosion. I was one of the first men in Nagasaki after the bomb was dropped. Few of the bodies I examined were so radioactive as these remains."

Palfrey's throat felt hot and dry.

"And there's no doubt?" he asked.

"None at all. The blood is radioactive to an alarming degree, and yet—" He gulped, and his lips were working. "Understand me, Palfrey. Anyone who touched that blood would suffer from the most acute wasting disease – a malignancy I cannot explain in terms of radioactivity. Walsh here —" Copuscenti turned almost despairingly to the other man—"has terrified me."

Walsh, the toxicologist ? Palfrey, puzzled until then by Copuscenti's fear, began to understand; and his own earlier doubts of the significance of the radioactivity were strengthened.

Walsh had a hard voice and a clipped way of speaking.

"I don't know what it is, Dr. Palfrey. I do know that the tissues of these—ah—things contain a substance that accounts for their phenomenal rate of growth. Phenomenal. I have dissected and analysed these tissues. They are, by human standards, malignant. Cancerous. And humans are vulnerable to this condition. One of my assistants has just died – three days after being infected by a creature's blood entering through a scratch on his finger. A second assistant is dying."

"*Now* you see why I am terrified," Copuscenti muttered.

Palfrey felt as if he were made of ice.

"I doubt if anyone who actually touched the blood could survive for more than a day or so," Dr. Walsh went on. "Whether it affects the atmosphere so that it can spread its poisonous effect widely, I don't yet know. There are indications that it does not, also indications that the skin of the creatures might be insulated so that there is no danger until the blood is spilt. I do not say this *is* so; only that it might be."

"Dreadful!" Copuscenti said.

Palfrey pulled the Geiger counter away, and the rattling stopped.

"Go on," he said flatly.

"The blood of the two people whom Walsh and I examined at Salisbury shows advanced stages of leukaemia, or blood cancer. One of them, your agent Anderson, recently underwent a routine medical examination in which a blood test was carried out. I have seen the report. There was no sign of leukaemia, nothing to suggest anything abnormal in his blood condition. The general health of the farmer who died was known to be excellent."

Palfrey's voice hardly sounded.

"Yes?"

"We have just finished a preliminary examination of the blood of two victims of the latest attack," Copuscenti went on. "There's evidence of leukaemia – very thin blood indeed. We are having hourly examinations made, and can report that the condition of the blood deteriorated rapidly in the first hour. I think you must accept that these animals cause a form of leukaemia when they poison human beings. The poison appears also to be secreted under the nails or the tips of the fingers, and can be injected through the talons.

"It is hideous—hideous. Far worse than smallpox or the bubonic plague."

"There is infinitely less chance of survival," Walsh went on. "This could develop into a world-wide epidemic which would create conditions even worse than those of nuclear explosion. *I am not exaggerating, Dr. Palfrey.* A scratch from those creatures does cause acute leukaemia. So does contact with their blood. And there appear to be great numbers of them."

Palfrey said stiffly: "I think there are."

"How many? Hundreds? Thousands?" demanded Copuscenti.

Palfrey thought: "There could be millions." He waved a hand. "We're trying to find out."

"Palfrey—I know of no defence against them," Copuscenti said.

"There is none," Walsh put in. "It is possible that infection can come by breathing in a few living cells from the creatures. Such people as you and I, with medical knowledge, can protect ourselves. The man in the street could not."

"I realise that," Palfrey said, stiffly. "If we attack them and cause bleeding, then the infection could begin, at once."

"Yes. And is deadly."

After a long time, Palfrey said almost in a sigh: "Gas."

"First find the creatures. We must know how many there are, Palfrey!" Copuscenti clenched his fists and glared, as if Palfrey were refusing to do what was so obviously necessary. "What plans have you?"

Palfrey thought: if he's so distraught, can he be objective enough to come with me to Lozania? And he thought: where did they come from? What created them? He looked dispassionately into Copuscenti's eyes.

"If we can find from where they originate, then we might stop them."

"At the source, you mean." Copuscenti said. "At source, perhaps." He closed his eyes and moved back a pace, and when he spoke again it was in a very different tone. "You shame me, Palfrey. I was so shocked, I felt as if I were going mad. But you are right. Where do they come from? They have human characteristics and human intelligence, Miss Morgan tells me. They are in the shape of humans. I have discussed this at some length with Dr. Campson, who confirms the anatomical closeness as we know them to human beings. Find where they come from, and perhaps you can stop them – but suppose they come from one of the other planets. We can now send our intelligent creatures through space. So it is no longer absurd to consider the possibility of intelligent human beings coming to us through space. What protection is there against such a contingency? Answer me that."

Very slowly Palfrey said. "Let's worry about that when we know for certain they don't come from somewhere on earth. I would like you to come with me to Lozania because ..."

Copuscenti listened, and finally he said: "Of course, I will come. I will have a little rest, and be ready whenever you wish. I shall want Dr. Walsh with me, if that is possible."

"Of course," Palfrey said.

"Thank you." Copuscenti actually smiled, more relaxed than he had been throughout the interview. Walsh nodded, jerkily. "You are good for me, Dr. Palfrey," went on the Professor. "You have a most calming effect. I think a discussion with you at least once a week would be the best therapy conceivable for me." He went to the door with Walsh, and unexpectedly shook hands with Palfrey.

Calming, thought Palfrey. Therapy.

As he went to his office, the full significance of everything the Professor and Dr. Walsh had said, swept over him. By the time he reached his desk, he was quivering with a physical reaction, and could hardly control the muscles of his mouth. He dropped into his chair, shivering. His forehead was damp with sweat, his whole body seemed to be drained of blood.

Drained of blood, as if he were suffering from leukaemia.

He buried his face in his hands, and was still like that when the door opened, and Joyce Morgan came in. He was aware of her, but did not look up, until he heard the door close. She had gone. He knew that she must be feeling much as he had felt when confronted with Copuscenti's first reaction. Her coming and going did a little to draw him out of his mood of shocked despair. He had given instructions before going to the laboratory, and she had put some notes on his desk. Everything was in hand; the aircraft had been laid on, there was an appointment with the British Prime Minister at ten o'clock before he left for the airport. An analysis of the reports from Z5 agents was there, too.

He began to study this, his mind working again, but he was aware that he was working at half-pressure. The news, added to what had already happened, had bruised his mind, so that he had lost the power of concentration which had set him apart from most men for so long.

There were forty-two reports from twenty-nine countries.

In twenty-two countries there were acute food shortages, caused almost without exception by losses ascribed to rats. Throughout the world, food storage warehouses and barns which had been untouched for months were being opened, and thousands of them were found empty – the grain and in other staple diets eaten by scavenging hordes. Every report seemed to tear savagely into Palfrey's screaming nerves. Such quantities of food would not have disappeared unless there had been enormous numbers of the creatures feeding off it.

Millions, many millions. He turned a page in the report and saw a typewritten note signed: 'A. J. Kent.' Kent was the best mathematician in Z5, and the code and cypher expert. His note read:

The skin of the creatures is very thin, and the ratio of the skin *area* to the stomach *volume* is five times greater than ours. They eat five times more than we do in relation to their size. Using this basis, and by totalling the amount of food consumed by them as far as we know, I estimate that at least five million are in existence. There could be a hundred million.

Palfrey closed his eyes and leaned back in his chair, so despairing that he could not think. The door opened again and he thought it was Joyce, and didn't immediately open his eyes. He heard her approach, and then suddenly heard her voice.

"Are you tired, Dr. Palfrey?"

It was Beth Fordham.

Chapter Twelve

THESE CREATURES MULTIPLY

Palfrey was startled for a moment, and his heart missed a beat. Then he said: "Beth" in a whisper only he could hear. She stood in front of him with that half-smile, a Mona Lisa kind of inscrutability, and did not seem to notice that he had said 'Beth' not 'Betty'. She was calm and rested – tiredness did not seem to affect her. She wore a suit, with a high collar, the cuffs low over her hands; he had no doubt that she had taken these precautions against the rabbit men.

"Yes," Palfrey said at last. "And I can't afford to be tired."

"You can afford to rest," she retorted.

Rest, he thought bitterly. How could one rest with so much on one's mind?

"You must rest," she went on, "or you'll crack up, and that won't help anybody."

He didn't answer at first, it was such a trite thing to say. Yet it was true, too, and her smile had a soothing effect. He was on the point of asking how she had got here when he changed his mind, and said: "Wait here a moment, will you?"

He went outside. A tall, red-haired agent who was always available as a messenger, stood aside. As the door closed, Palfrey touched a one-way window in the passage; he could see exactly what 'Beth' was doing. Why did he think of her as Beth? He went into Joyce's office, and as that door closed, asked sharply, "How did Mrs. Fordham get into my office?"

"I sent her in," Joyce answered.

"She hasn't been approved yet. That was folly."

"Perhaps it was," Joyce conceded. She stood up from her desk. As always she seemed taller than he expected. "Sap, you looked dreadful when I came in."

"I felt dreadful."

"You looked nearly as bad this morning."

"Must I put on a mask for you?"

Joyce said quietly: "Sap, a year ago it would have hurt me terribly if you'd talked like that, but it doesn't now. I know you, and you know that I've been in love with you for a long time. I think I've come to know what you need. I really do."

Only half-mollified, Palfrey said, "You fuss over me as if I were a pet dog."

"Perhaps I do." She was determined to be conciliatory. "Sap, please listen to me. I've never known you so affected by a case. You sensed the magnitude of it from the beginning – you have this awful prescience. And it's done something to you. It's sapped a lot of your strength, you must know that."

How well he knew it!

"Yet you've never needed all your strength and single-mindedness as you do now." Joyce continued. "As we do now."

Palfrey asked more quietly: "What has all this to do with Mrs. Fordham?"

"A great deal," Joyce said. "I was startled to see you so relaxed when you came back from her this morning. It didn't last long, but it was astonishing. Mrs. Fordham did something to you, actually gave you back some of the strength you'd lost. Didn't you sense that?"

He had indeed, but could he admit it now? Wasn't it absurd to believe that he could draw strength from a woman whom he had known for only a few hours? He began to coil strands of hair about his forefinger and slowly his lips curved in a smile.

"I suppose I did," he said. "But she's still a grave security risk."

"You'll be a bigger one, if you can't stand up to the strain. And it's going to get worse. Sap ..." Joyce rounded the desk and came towards him taking his hands; she was very close and very attractive in her earnestness. "The last thing I want is for you to find comfort with another woman. I always hoped it would be with me. But I know now, it won't be. Take her with you to Lozan. If you do, you may be able to rest on the flight, instead of sleeping under drugs which take the edge off your mind. You need natural sleep, natural relaxation. Take her with you." When he didn't answer, Joyce went on: "She isn't *such* a big security risk. All the inquiries we've made are in her favour. If she were being considered as an agent, we would feel by now she would be all right. Even Armitage's report is good."

"How well does he know her?"

"He lunched with her," Joyce said simply. "And I spent an hour with her, too. Tig said he thought she was as good as bread."

Palfrey almost exclaimed aloud.

"And if you want to know more about her, here's the report so far," Joyce went on. "She's forty-four, one of five children of a Devonshire farmer, who made a lot of money. She was educated at Malvem College for Girls and a year at the Sorbonne in Paris. She was going to read philosophy and economics at Girton, but her mother fell ill, and she stayed at home, housekeeping, for two years. That was when she met David Fordham. The reports say it was a love match. There were two children. One died of poliomyelitis, the other was drowned in a boating accident. All of her sisters and brothers are alive, married, and as far as we can tell from a quick check, highly reputable. One solicitor, one farmer, one shopkeeper's wife, one a parson's wife. All of them live in the South-West."

Joyce stopped, and drew back.

Palfrey laughed; and it was a long time since he had felt like laughing.

"Will you take her?" Joyce asked eagerly.

"Yes," Palfrey answered. "I'll give your amateur psychiatry a chance." His eyes shone. "In any case I like her!"

"That's why I think she'll be good for you," Joyce Morgan said.

Palfrey laughed again.

Yet as he left Joyce's office, he sobered up at once, with a new
and different kind of problem; how to tell Beth Fordham why he
wanted to take her to Lozan? She had offered, in fact begged to
help, but this was hardly what she had asked to be – a course in
therapy for Stanislaus Alexander Palfrey. He laughed again, and
turned to the messenger.

"Anything?"

"She took a book down from the right-hand case, and has been
looking through it. She didn't go nearer your desk."

"All right, thanks." Palfrey went in, and immediately Betty
Fordham looked up, with a slightly preoccupied air, as if suddenly
she wondered where she was.

"Hallo."

"Hallo," said Palfrey. "What are you reading?"

"Russell's *Conquest of Happiness.*"

Palfrey almost gaped.

"With the world falling to pieces about you?"

She laughed. "If I have to die, I'd rather die happy." She stopped
speaking, and a dark thought had obviously crossed her mind.
"Did that sound callous? I'm sorry if it did, but I think my husband
was happy. In fact I'm sure he was. And I never could live in the
past."

"Yesterday's past always seems a long way away," remarked
Palfrey gently. He stood in front of her, taking the book. "My wife
would have enjoyed knowing you," he said, his eyes crinkling at
the corners. "And my secretary thinks you are good for me."

"Does she?" Eagerness lit up Beth's eyes. "Oh, I'm so glad. And
I do hope she's right."

"So do I," said Palfrey drily. "Will you think me absurd if I call
you Beth, not Betty?"

"Of course not."

"Thank you," Palfrey stared at her for what seemed a long time,
and there was a kind of peace inside him; at least temporary
freedom from the awful turmoil which had been so agonising a
short while before. "We think we have a clue about the origin of
these creatures."

Beth waited, her breathing quickening.

"In Lozan. I'm to fly out there tonight, with a small team of investigators."

Still she kept silent.

"Will you come?" Palfrey asked.

"If you think I'll be useful."

"I would like you to come."

"Then of course I will," she said.

Palfrey moved away and sat on the edge of his desk, still looking at her, and still puzzled by this unexpected peace. Beth's expression was calm and interested. He had the strange idea that although she grasped what he had said she did not see the full implication; there was an unsophisticated simplicity about her.

"You'll need to study reports which won't make nice reading," he said. "They can't be much nastier than the things I've seen."

"That's true enough," Palfrey conceded. "Can you be ready by half past twelve."

"Of course."

"I'll see you then," he said. "Here."

She gave a rather wistful smile, perhaps a little mechanical, or perhaps more truly puzzled, and went out. He picked up his telephone and told Joyce to let her see the Copuscenti and Walsh reports, the Campson autopsy report and the analysis of the reports from overseas. That done, he began to read the analysis again. The horror was no less, but the effect on him was quite different; it was as if Beth Fordham acted on him as a sedative. Whatever the cause, he could now think more clearly and objectively. If one ignored the leukaemia danger, one must try to estimate the amount of food already eaten, and how many people it would affect. If there were ten million eating that amount of food dally— and if they multiplied quickly, obviously they would greatly aggravate the shortages in countries where there was already a food problem.

One such place was Lozania.

"What do you expect to find in Lozania, Palfrey?" asked the Prime Minister.

"I hope, information of these creatures."

"What do you think of the Copuscenti and Walsh reports?"

"Accurate," Palfrey answered.

"Yes. If the consumption of food goes on at the present rate, how long do you think stocks will last?"

"We don't know how long the present situation has been developing. If they are infested by the creatures, the food situation in China, the Far East generally, India and Pakistan and some South American countries could be grave within two months."

"Or less."

Palfrey said slowly: "I should have said acute in two months. It's grave now."

"And Europe?"

"It will depend on the harvest," Palfrey reasoned, but there was no conviction in his voice.

The Prime Minister moved away and studied the analysis again. In a voice as flat as Palfrey's he said: "I have analysed and studied all the reports. It is now known that there are seventy-five colonies under the earth, much the same as the one you first discovered. If these creatures get hungry they will steal the food before it is harvested."

"That's another of my fears, sir."

"My God!" Mason said, as if the horror suddenly struck home. "My God, if we can't kill them, what are we going to do? How many are there? How can we possibly cope? The War Minister suggests gas, but how can we gas these creatures without gassing the people? Palfrey—" Mason caught his breath. "Is there a chance? Or have we discovered this situation too late? Even without them the world food problem is acute. The World Food Organisation prophesies four major famine areas next year – Southern China, North-East India, Pakistan and Indonesia. Others will be on the borderline. If these creatures multiply, the famine will come much sooner even than we feared. We simply have to stop their breeding and multiplying, we have to find a way of saving the food for the people already in the world. Do you think you might have a real hope in Lozania?"

"As far as I can judge, it's the only hope we have," Palfrey said soberly. "I wish—"

There was a tap at the door of this small room at Number 10, and the Prime Minister looked across in annoyance, but called: "Come in." A middle aged man entered, austere-looking, grave.

"I'm sorry to worry you, sir, but there is an urgent telephone message for Dr. Palfrey, from Smolensk."

Immediately Palfrey's thought sprang to Stephan Andromovitch, the Russian who was second in Command of Z5.

Andromovitch was a huge man, six feet seven tall, broad, massive, a giant in size as well as in achievement. He had been for many years almost the only reliable source of communication between East and West, the only man trusted by Moscow and Peking as well as by Washington and Whitehall. Of late, Palfrey had been accepted too, and regular channels of communication had been opened. There was at least a measure of trust in many spheres.

No one who saw Andromovitch for the first time was surprised at the faith he inspired. He had big features, inevitably, and undoubtedly he was handsome, but it was his expression, at times almost beautiful, which broke down the barriers of prejudice and distrust. Many a hard-bitten, sophisticated, even callous journalist had described the giant Russian as having the face of a saint.

On the day when Palfrey had been in the centre of the situation in London, at the time of the horror in Piccadilly, Andromovitch had been in one of the richest wheat-producing areas in Western Russia, not far from the Polish border. He had been summoned by a Z5 agent who was a Party Member and leader of the Commune of Istra which had thrice won a prize for growing the finest crops in the Soviet Union. This year, the wheat had promised to be exceptional, even for Istra. That afternoon, Andromovitch had stood with a silent crowd of peasants, seeing how vast fields of wheat had been eaten down to the stubble. There could be no harvest here, the crop had gone.

There was worse.

Towards the east, where the land rose in gentle slopes, some earth subsidence had been discovered and with a company of Red Star Army, Andromovitch had investigated, and had used cyanide gas, as on vermin.

Everyone had stood, appalled.

Here was a primitive underground city, like the one near Salisbury in England, but with one dreadful difference. All the inhabitants were dying, or dead, the young outnumbering their parents by tens of thousands.

"I saw these things myself, Sap," Stefan Andromovitch said in a hard voice. "I saw women who had died as they gave birth. I saw seven of the females who had been delivered of *ten* young. The average litter, and that is the only word I can think of, was eight.

"These creatures multiply ten-fold with each generation."

Chapter Thirteen

THE MOUNTAIN OF HORROR

"Your Excellency," said the Lozanian interpreter, "I have the honour to present Dr. Palfrey."

"Doctor."

"Excellency."

"And Mrs. Fordham."

"Madame."

"I'm glad to meet you, Mr. President."

"Mr. Andromovitch."

"Mr. President."

"Professor Copuscenti."

The Professor, perhaps more tense than any of those present, bowed stiffly.

The introductions, at the Palace of the Hills, overlooking the great Bay of Lozania, took less than five minutes. Copuscenti gave the impression that he thought every second was wasted. Stefan Andromovitch seemed the least troubled, the most composed, and Beth Fordham glanced at him continually, in wonder or in awe. The President, a silver-haired handsome man with bright, dark eyes and a high-bridged nose, bore the reputation of a benevolent dictator, his neo-Fascist leanings long part of the international scene. Once looked for, the resemblance between him and the tiny creatures was as noticeable as that between them and Taza.

Palfrey gave an involuntary shiver of apprehension.

"Mr. President," he said at last, "the matter is urgent."

"This I know," said the President. "Dr. Palfrey, there are some matters I would prefer to discuss with you alone."

"I would have to tell my colleagues immediately, sir."

"I agreed to the ambassador's request that I should acquaint you of certain facts only if they could be kept in confidence."

Copuscenti was glaring at the President, his hands clenching and unclenching.

"Your Excellency," Palfrey said, "if we cannot find the truth about these creatures, quickly, the world will perish. Your name, your country's name, will have no significance if that should happen. If we can avoid identifying you or Lozania, we will – but if you have to be named so as to give us a chance of survival, then I shall name you."

"Time!" Copuscenti breathed. "Every minute matters."

"Dr. Palfrey," said the President in his excellent English, "we are a small nation and we have been dependent on the largesse of our wealthier neighbours for a long time. We have few natural sources of wealth or energy, and the cost of nuclear power was far beyond our economy. We had the assistance of both Russian and German physicists. We worked along different lines from those of other nations. We discovered a method of carrying out certain limited experiments, even of nuclear weapons, without them being detected. We were confident of the success of our endeavours but the nuclear reactor research station was closely guarded. We selected a place which was accessible from the mainland and yet was far enough away to be cut off if anything went wrong. I speak, of course, of the Isle of Lozan."

Palfrey could picture the island in his mind's eye. It was two or three miles off the coast, in the middle of the magnificent bay, a rocky island which had seemed ugly and bare of vegetation, a derelict jewel in the vivid blue of the sea.

"We flew over it," Copuscenti muttered. "Get on, get on."

"During the two world wars we have used the Island of Lozan for storing our precious inheritances – our art treasures, our historical relics, our records – everything. There are three secret tunnels from the mainland to the island."

Palfrey had known there were such tunnels, but no more.

"When we began our nuclear research and our experiments we worked on the Isle," the President went on. "All our hopes were vested in it. We made it a self-sufficient underground city with huge food stocks and supplies of all kinds. If anything happened above ground, we believed the underground city would be safe."

After a pause, the President continued: "Five times we carried out undetected tests of defensive weapons which appeared to be wholly successful. We housed two thousand families on the Isle, in an underground city which had every amenity we could give it, to provide both nuclear energy and nuclear weapons. We also had some research laboratories – we were studying the effect of radiation on such diseases as cancer and leukaemia."

Palfrey had vivid pictures of the subterranean city near Salisbury and the other near Smolensk. He did not speak, and none of the others spoke, each fascinated by what this grave-faced, austere man was saying. Palfrey was aware of Beth's arm touching his – both with assurance and for assurance.

"These families were to stay on the island until the work had been finished, and we had reached our objective – *nuclear power,* the solution to our economic ills and our pitiful standard of living—"

Suddenly the President broke off, turned away and pressed a button on his desk. A whirring sound followed, and a large white screen dropped down over one of the windows. On a table opposite to this was a movie projector already loaded. The President moved across to it.

"Please bring chairs."

"Have we time—" Copuscenti began.

Palfrey's hand tightened on his arm, silencing him. Andromovitch picked up a heavy chair in each hand, the others took one each.

"Because of the vital importance of security we had the island of Lozan watched by television and cine cameras, all equipped with sound recording attachments," the President continued. "All the approaches were covered, and television and film cameras were placed at strategic points through the reactor station, which was built on several subterranean levels beneath the island. There was an underground city with all facilities for communal and family life, as well as the factory or research establishment, where the workers lived. Do you follow?"

"Clearly," Palfrey said, and Andromovitch said: "Most certainly."

"These cameras were all under electronic control, and movement was sufficient to operate them. Some were in action all day, and the closed circuit television was watched every minute. Each day, too, the film was brought here and studied. Any suspicious movement would be detected at once. I am about to show you of what happened on the second day of April, this year – four months and five days ago.

"After you have seen the pictures, there will be other films, which have been edited so that they present the story of events chronologically. A moment please, while I switch off the lights."

He moved away; there was a click, and darkness dropped into the room. A moment later the beam from the projector pierced the dark, and the date April 2nd 196- appeared on the screen. Immediately afterwards a picture of the Isle of Lozan appeared in vivid colour, quite beautiful with its surf – and sand – ringed beaches, its inlets, its cliffs, the rich vegetation on the rocky slopes, the white houses, the children playing in or near the water, the mothers watching. The island was surrounded by deep water, big ships were in the channel between it and the port of Lozan, where a cruise ship gay with flags, and garlanded with flowers, was moving slowly from the dockside.

Copuscenti gasped: "I remember! I remember, the earthquake …"

To him, to Palfrey, to them all, what followed was not only hideous and horrible, but so vivid that it felt as if they were living through the awful day itself, and the weeks which followed.

All was peace and beauty on the island and in the Bay of Lozan on that lovely April day, when the sun shone and the wind blew.

Then, suddenly, the water at one side of the island erupted.

One moment, there was the idyllic scene; next it was blotted out by a great wall of water, and as this rose, the whole island vanished except for the top of the mountain. In a few seconds, an enormous tidal wave crashed with uncontrollable fury, swallowing up small craft and large. The sky turned dark. The cruise ship, so majestic for so long, was struck with such force that it was lifted out of the water and flung onto the quayside. As suddenly it was engulfed, swallowed in the mighty wave with all buildings and other ships nearby.

There was left only the horror ...

The picture changed, to show the aftermath, a sultry sea, and on its bosom the wreckage of large craft and small, and the bodies of countless men and women and children. There was a great pall in the sky, hiding the sun, casting a red, sullen glow over the water.

One side of the island had vanished into the sea. The other remained, as it appeared today; dead and desolate.

As Palfrey and the others watched, appalled, the scene changed to pictures inside the island fortress, underground. They saw an underground city, far larger than that which Palfrey had seen near Salisbury, and Andromovitch near Smolensk; but much the same, with huge dormitories, communal kitchens, communal recreation rooms, a cinema, a theatre, nurseries – and in one place, new born babies with their mothers, a woman in the very act of giving birth.

The picture seemed to break; one moment everything was normal, the next it was as if everything was hurled into the air, in fire and smoke and awful bedlam. And the screaming rose to a terrible pitch ...

Slowly, the smoke settled; and faded – like the mist had done on Salisbury Plain.

The President said huskily: "Not all the cameras were destroyed."

On the screen there appeared the date: *April 30th.*

After it, there came a different picture, a kind of miniature, like a child's model of the city they had seen destroyed in front of their eyes. The picture covered the same area, but ten, a hundred times more was crowded into it, and instead of the magnificent underground city it was primitive and rough. There were people, too; tiny people.

They moved about, near-naked, with a controlled busyness. No one smiled, or relaxed, or talked; instead, each group went about its work with a controlled application and energy which was appalling in itself; for these were tiny creatures; ant-like; yet they were midget humans, behaving as if they were trained to every movement and terrified in case they failed to do what they were there to do. Among them were a few slightly taller creatures who behaved as if with authority.

The picture changed.

Palfrey saw what Andromovitch had seen; the new-born in litters of eight and nine and ten. And he saw 'children' fully grown; and the food stocks almost gone; great warehouses empty.

Copuscenti gasped: "In four weeks. Four *weeks*. It can't be."

"You see it as it happened," the President said. "And look."

Next, ordinary men approached the tiny city, men wearing masks and equipped with all the protective clothing of anyone going into a radiation area; and yet the tiny creatures, near-naked, lived and thrived.

"No!" screamed Copuscenti.

Palfrey felt Beth's fingers tighten on his arm, and could imagine how she felt, for suddenly two of the creatures sprang upon the ordinary men, and rent their clothing and tore at their throats, killing them.

The picture changed.

It was hideous beyond words, for the tiny creatures, once with plenty of room to move in, were now jammed tight in every nook and cranny, wriggling like maggots. Palfrey felt sick. Copuscenti groaned. Andromovitch said: "It cannot be." Beth turned her face away. Walsh sat staring, lips working.

And the seething, writhing mass of living creatures grew larger and larger.

They spread out through the rock. They tunnelled with tiny tools powered by some energy Palfrey did not understand. They reached the side of the mountain and the sea. They ate everything in their path. They swam, but few if any drowned. They were like a great shoal of fish, wriggling and writhing. And gradually they spread out, moving to every point on the compass, until at last they disappeared, and the sea was calm.

The projector stopped, and the silence was unbroken for what seemed a long, long time.

Then the President said: "I cannot show you what followed, Dr. Palfrey, but our greatest nuclear physicist, who escaped the disaster, can tell you all he knows."

Chapter Fourteen

"... OUT OF IGNORANCE AND FOLLY ..."

The man who came into the room was short and very broad. His face was small, and like that of a very old man, although there was youthful vigour in his body, and in the firmness of his grip as he shook hands with Palfrey, Copuscenti and Walsh. He nodded to the others as the President said: "Dr. Severini, I have told them everything I can up to the last days of the exodus." The President's voice had an edge of weariness. "You understand it was only six weeks ago, Dr. Palfrey."

"I understand," Palfrey said.

"It is unbelievable," said Andromovitch.

"*Cancer* research," Walsh rasped.

"Six weeks—and they are now in every part of the world," Copuscenti said in a hoarse voice.

"The period of gestation is nine days," Dr. Severini announced in good but heavily accented English. "We isolated four pairs, very early after the first discovery, and allowed them to mate. The result was phenomenal, quite phenomenal. Within ten days, from the four couples, there were thirty-seven young, one odd female whom the parents killed and ate – there is other evidence that they are cannibalistic, although their preference appears to be for small vermin, insects and birds, even small animals. They also eat large quantities of vegetable foods, fruits, and particularly, sugar. The young become fertile in fourteen days. As far as I can tell, there was a polygamous society—what do you say in England? Farmyard morals?"

He paused for comment.

"Farmyard morals," Beth echoed huskily.

"So. Fifteen days after the birth of the first thirty-seven young, there were one hundred and sixty-three in the generation, or two hundred and seven including the first four pairs. Twenty-five days later, there were nearly seventeen hundred. They devoured all the food within the area; stripped two fields of corn, and then burrowed into the earth. We lost trace of them. They carry tiny supplies of dried leaves, which gives off smoke when burned. The smoke hides them. They ate their way across the southern tip of Lozania, and into the mountains – and none appear to have returned." There was a pause in the monologue, one in which no one stirred. "I hoped that they would be unable to survive at certain altitudes and low temperatures, and certainly they disappeared. Our researches in the waters off the coast showed that many thousands had drowned, and I gave the President reasonable ground for hope that all of them had perished in the sea. Until—" he broke off.

Palfrey's eyes were closed as he tried to take this in.

"I have a report from a professor of the Department of Physics at the Lozan University," Severini went on. "Observation has shown that about half of the average litter are females. Whether each female produces one or several litters is not significant in view of what is known of the fecundity. The Professor states that the population of the creatures will multiply by ten, in thirty-eight days, by one hundred in seventy-six days, and by one thousand in one hundred and fourteen days. So if the world has ten million now, in four months it will have ten thousand million of these creatures, or at least two for every human being. Beyond that, I cannot begin to comprehend, for they will multiply rapidly, soon covering all the world's surface, land and sea."

No one spoke when he paused, and he went on again: "We have discovered that there are two degrees of intelligence and intellectual development in the creatures, much the same as in human beings.

A few are brilliant technicians, and natural leaders. They have perfected a simple method of creating and using their energy but they need enormous quantities of food. They imitate human beings in most behaviour patterns and I believe much of this imitation is inbred. They can think, and yet they do foolish things. The leaders – sometimes the killers – soon lose their self-control, and often kill for the sake of killing. On the other hand they are highly protective to their own weaker brothers."

Severini broke off again and looked appealingly at the President.

"Dr. Palfrey," President Mortini said, with an obvious effort. "I devoutly hoped – all of us hoped – that the creatures had all perished. We heard no reports of them. My ambassadors throughout the world were instructed to keep the closest watch. So were our Intelligence agents. No word reached us until your discovery and the request for information from Z5."

"Why didn't you give it at once?" Palfrey demanded.

The handsome face took on an expression of infinite sadness.

"I do not expect anyone to understand the horror I felt at such news. The sense of shame. The awful responsibility. I consulted Dr. Severini when I heard from Clemente Taza. He told me what I am sure is true – it would be a matter of days before you were aware of the nature and fecundity of these creatures. We could do no positive good. We hoped we might avoid admission of our responsibility. But some of the young, it now appears, were carried in the baggage of one of our diplomats in London. They were highly intelligent specimens. We do not know for certain, but we believe they were searching for new areas to colonise. They realise how desperately they will need to expand the land they live off, but they do not appear to have given a moment's thought to any form of birth-control."

Beth said in a hushed voice: "Nor did we, until it was nearly too late."

The President said quietly: "In South America, we have been more guilty than most countries about over-population, but—" He caught his breath. "Before we could stop them, they escaped, and we know that a colony grew beneath the house. An attempt to gas them failed. In the course of it we discovered that some of the creatures have this high intelligence and are able to communicate among themselves. Also they were travelling freely to and from the Embassy. The colonies are not wholly autonomous, there is some kind of communication between them. At some stage, presumably for protection, some assumed rabbit, cat and dog skins – and we now know that the fighters among them use a fur disguise."

Palfrey moved across the room, twisting a strand of hair about his finger.

"They certainly have a high intelligence, with blank patches of sheer stupidity," he said. "They have means of communication. They have scouts or fighters, to protect the colonies. They have engineers who build beneath the earth, and how they eat! Do you know what tools they use for building?"

"We believe that most of them are manual, but some are automatic, charged by the stupendous energy each one stores in the body," said Severini. "We have tried to kill them by atomic radiation but they are quite immune to it. They have this abnormal physical strength."

"Abnormal indeed!" cried Copuscenti. "Do you know the obvious truth, Palfrey?"

"There are so many," Palfrey said. "Which one do you consider paramount?"

"That each of the creatures is powered by a built-in source of atomic energy. That is why they can work as they do, that explains their abnormal physical strength and their unbelievable staying power. To *swim* the South Atlantic, and the other great oceans – what physical strength they must have!"

Dr. Walsh's eyes were bright with excitement when he cut across Copuscenti's words.

"The research into cancer and leukaemia, the existence of sufferers from the diseases in the city would explain the malignancy of the tissues of the creatures," he said. "It would explain why all of them are carriers of the malignant germ-cells in the blood, perhaps in the breath.

"The poisoning takes place only when the blood is exposed to the air," Dr. Severini said. "Similarly, the nuclear energy is in the blood, generated in a way not yet known. Once there is bleeding the energy is dissipated – and it dissipates on death too. If they multiply at such a rate—" he broke off, almost choked by his own words and the horror of the facts.

Palfrey said flatly: "What are the figures and facts beyond those we already know?"

"The Professor's report is comprehensive and thorough on the known *data*," declared Severini. "The figures are of course dependent on certain facts not yet known, because we have not been able to study the behaviour of the creatures over a long enough period. If half of each litter are in fact, females, and each female lives for several generations, mating again immediately on parturition, or carrying enough sperm from the first mating to fertilise a series of batches of ova, or is parthenogenic, and produces a litter every nine days, similar statistics hold. The population will multiply by ten about every twenty-six days, by a hundred every fifty-three days, by a thousand every seventy-five days. So, as we said before, an increase from ten million of the creatures to a thousand million would take fifty-three days, and the increase to a million million would take one hundred and thirty-two days. Whether the present estimate of ten million in existence is accurate or not makes little difference. Even if the starting figure was only ten thousand, the million million would be reached within two hundred and twelve days – or seven months."

As he stopped, the only sound was the harsh breathing of the others, until Beth said: "So even if they do not infect us, we cannot stop them from eating us out of existence."

"Even if we could we couldn't prevent them from driving us into the sea," Palfrey said bleakly. "A million million of them would need to occupy an enormous area. Are there any statistics available on that?"

"Yes," answered Severini. "If they had a square foot each – such a tiny space! – they would need thirty thousand square miles – more than half of England, Dr. Palfrey – mountain and valley, good land and bad included."

"There would be a solid mass blotting out all London, all of Southern England from the Humber to the mouth of the Severn," Palfrey said heavily.

Beth was holding his arm very tightly.

"That is so," agreed Severini. "And now there are positive figures. If you can imagine these creatures in one circular patch, they would move out from the extreme fringe at the rate of four miles a day. Seventy-six days later they would cover three million square miles – all of North America except the North-West territories of Canada."

"It would take less than a year to cover the whole land area of the earth," said Andromovitch. And he shivered.

"And they did not all drown," muttered Copuscenti.

"Not all of them would drown when they were pushed off the land masses," agreed Severini.

"So not only could they starve us to death, but they could take up all our living space," Palfrey said in a husky voice. "They could take over the world."

"Unless they are stopped, then inevitably they will," declared Andromovitch.

"What hope is there of stopping them?" demanded Beth, in a quivering voice.

Not one man answered.

Beth caught her breath.

"That horrible picture," she said.

"Which one?"

"The one when they looked like maggots."

"Well?"

"The whole world will be like that if they're not stopped. Don't you realise? They'll be worse than termites, worse than any insect, and they'll devour everything."

Dr. Severini let out a long, slow, softly-hissing breath.

Palfrey unwound the strands of hair and smoothed them into the familiar flaxen curve.

"First things first. In a few months, they can create famine conditions anywhere in the world, that's unarguable. Dr. Severini—"
"Yes?"
"Do you know of any way of killing them, except by methods which draw blood?"
"I do not."
"There is cyanide of potassium when they are in a confined space," Andromovitch said, "but that cannot be used without grave risk to people. Moreover, the early reports from Russian pathologists state that death was by suffocation caused by the gas, not by the poison itself. It is not practical except in small concentrated doses, or in huge underground cities. On the surface we cannot use gasses."
"No." Palfrey said.
"We must capture a hundred, a thousand of these creatures," Copuscenti said hotly. "We must capture enough to use every known gas and poison, until we find out what will kill them, and yet be harmless to human beings."
"If there is such a thing." Severini said despairingly.
"We must find a way of destroying them!" Copuscenti was beside himself.
Severini said heavily: "If we are to survive as a human race, yes. However, there is no law which guarantees our survival, is there? The world has been afraid of destruction by nuclear warfare, but, perhaps, *this* is going to lead to the end of the human race. Not by nuclear explosion, not by radiation, but simply by starvation – by famine. Be sure of this. If these creatures multiply at such a rate, the world will not have enough food to last for another year, perhaps not enough for six months. There are some of us who believed that the world would die of famine conditions in less than fifty years, unless the growth of population were strictly controlled. Unless these *Lozi* are destroyed—"
"*Lozi?*" ejaculated Palfrey.
"It is the name we have given them," Severini informed him. "Unless they can be destroyed, the world will starve in one year instead of fifty. You are right, Dr. Palfrey. They will devour the

animal food and all vegetable food, and clearly there is a danger that they might be able to eat and digest the organic part out of the topsoil, leaving a sterile desert. The danger to food is more acute than the danger to living space." Palfrey felt ice-cold.

"They must be killed," said Copuscenti, his voice hushed by the enormity of what was being said.

"We cannot use gas. We cannot shed their blood, or the infection will kill the human race. Asphyxiation is impossible *en masse,* once they are above ground." Severini was looking at Palfrey. "This is our dilemma, Dr. Palfrey. I do not envy you the task of resolving it."

"No. I don't suppose you do." Palfrey said drily.

"If you hadn't—" Beth began, but stopped.

Stefan Andromovitch spoke in his gentle voice, his face more like the face of a saint than ever.

"No kind of explanation can alter the truth, or conspire to mitigate it. If you had not carried out these secret nuclear tests, Mr. President, the situation might never have arisen."

President Mortini said bleakly: "We intended no harm. We did not dream of what would happen."

"You were under obligation, by international agreement, not to carry out independent experiments of this kind," Andromovitch declared coldly.

"Mr. Andromovitch," Severini said, with an edge to his voice. "This could have come about at any time. A single test, even at an atomic research station, would have released the form of radiation which has given life to these creatures. It was always known that radiation would have a genetic effect. We anticipated idiocy, disease, malformation and other freak births – that was the great argument of those who advocated banning the bomb. This is a different kind of genetic effect, one not anticipated. If we had not started it—"

"Specious nonsense!" Copuscenti interrupted angrily. "You are responsible and you know it. You, as a scientist, first, your president as a politician with dictatorial power, second. You're each culpable. My God! I—"

"That's more than enough," Palfrey interrupted.

"It isn't enough!" The physicist was red with emotion and barely suppressed rage. "This is no time for beating about the bush. We can't cope—we're finished. Done for. The human race is done for, I tell you. And all because men in authority would not accept their responsibility. That's the bloody truth of it."

"Your Excellency," Dr. Severini said icily, "there is no need for you to be subjected to such insult."

"Insult? If the truth is insulting, then it's time you heard it."

"Or what you know as the truth," Palfrey said. "Half the ills of the world would never have come about if people had realised what they were doing when they were doing it. There's nothing new about the failure to accept responsibility. If we all accepted ours all the time we would have much less to worry about."

"We've plenty to worry about now," Copuscenti growled.

"Yes. Our responsibilities. All of us, not to moralise, or cast blame. Yours specially to get ready to experiment on the *Lozi* with poisons and gases. Mine to find out how many colonies there are in the world, and how long the food supplies will last in each area. Dr. Walsh's – to try to find a way to immunise human beings against the malignancy. Every military authority's – the responsibility of capturing as many of the creatures as they can for experimental purposes. I've another – to get back to England and send out a general report." He hesitated, and then actually smiled at President Mortini. "Mr. President, I am not sure whether the world need know how the *Lozi* began – not yet at all events."

"You're very kind," Mortini said stiffly. "However I am going to broadcast to the world, Dr. Palfrey. There is nothing more to be served by hiding the facts. You will have to advise UNO, and the World Health Organisation to prepare for severe shortages of food. Food must be husbanded from this moment on. I will make a statement on television tonight. May I suggest that you help me prepare my speech?"

"If you wish," Palfrey said, and turned to Andromovitch. "Will you look after the other messages, Stefan? That we need some of these *Lozi* urgently but they mustn't be injured in any way which might make them bleed?"

"I will do that," Andromovitch said.

He left Palfrey and the President together.

Seven hours later, Andromovitch, Beth, Palfrey and his party were flying back to England. Copuscenti and Walsh had left earlier, to make all the necessary preparation; the request for living specimens of the *Lozi* had already gone out. Reports of newly discovered colonies had come in by the dozen; it was almost impossible to keep count.

Palfrey, Beth and Andromovitch sat together in the military aircraft, listening to a radio pick-up of Mortini's television speech. Palfrey could imagine the handsome face, the sadness, the self-reproach. He had known this man only for a few hours, yet had recognised in him the quality of greatness. This very quality had led to a disaster so awful that even Palfrey did not yet fully comprehend.

Mortini was saying: "It is a simple fact that I, like so many other patriots before me, placed the interests of my own country before those of the rest of the world. We ignored the advice of other great leaders of men, one of whom is Dr. Palfrey of whom I have already spoken. These men of vision warned us that each nation was dependent on its neighbours, just as each human being is dependent on other human beings.

"So, every man and woman on this planet is in danger, because of my mistaken patriotism. I am truly sorry.

"The truth now, as you will be told very often, is that time is needed desperately. The question is, whether there will be enough food for human-kind and for these parasites who now live off the earth. There is no danger left of nuclear war – for these parasites are proof against nuclear attack. So, the danger is that we may starve, because there are too many mouths to feed.

"I did not mean to release this horror upon the world. I did it out of ignorance and folly. I do not ask forgiveness, for it is too great a sin to forgive. What I do ask, what I beg of you, is that from this moment on you do everything in your power to prevent these parasitic demons from multiplying. And this you can do only by obeying the orders of those in authority.

"In this dreadful adversity, the world is as one. The shortage of food because of this phenomenal growth of an unwanted population truly makes all men brothers. My last wish is that mankind may survive the horror which has befallen it, and will emerge in a world truly at peace."

He stopped.

The jet engines droned on.

There was a sharp report from the radio, and a gasp.

"He has killed himself," Andromovitch said heavily.

"Oh, dear God," Beth said, in a hopeless voice. "Dear God."

Chapter Fifteen

THE BEGINNING OF THE FAMINE

The famine began in a tiny corner of India.

It began as famines have begun since the beginning of the world, with the failure of rice crops due to a typhoon.

There were no reserves of food to avoid the crisis.

The wind hurtled and cavorted, whirled and roared, and the rain hissed and smashed and pattered and turned even the dry uplands to mud. The floods submerged the young rice and tore it from the soil and carried it into the new- made rivers of rain into the swollen rivers from the mountains of the Himalayas. And as the waters ran into the sea, the horror was born.

The local stores of rice and wheat were also destroyed.

With the floods, came the creatures from the secret subterranean cities, whom the world now called the *Lozi*. The stores they had stolen from the paddy fields were gone, and the water was flooding their cities, so they were driven out of the earth by the fear of the floods and the fear of starvation, and they emerged to a land already ravaged by nature at her most violent, to a people stunned and shocked and hungry and helpless.

Here and there a village had its stores of food intact. As each long line of famished men and women and children gathered, the creatures came. At first the killer *Lozi*, attacking and terrifying, scattered the waiting crowds, the helpers and the helpless; and then the hordes descended like locusts, devouring all the food there was, and passed on still hungry, still ravening.

As they spread over the flooded earth, they ravaged. As they came to villages, they ravaged. As they came to the uplands they ate the green crops of corn and tea, of citrous fruits, of beans and all the foods of the earth. They left behind them the devastation of the floods and the devastation of their passing, and they did not burrow into the earth until they had sated themselves in a gluttony never known to man.

They covered an area as large as the State of New York, thrice the size of England, and soon disease was rife. There were the familiar diseases: smallpox, cholera, yellow fever, typhoid; and there was the new sickness which fell upon those whose blood was thinned after the creatures had bitten and clawed them. Many teams of rescue workers went in by air and road and rail, and for the time being, the famine was eased, but those who even touched the blood, or garments soiled by it, were ravaged by the leukaemia, and quickly died.

The next famine was in Southern China, in the province of Canton.

As the *Lozi* came out of their subterranean cities, they found a land scarred by the sun, the crops failing, the people already hungry and despairing. The dreadful pattern was repeated. Refugees fled out of the famine stricken land over the border fence and the dried up river which led to Hong Kong. The people of Hong Kong, already overcrowded, remained cheerful and confident, for they had survived countless crises before.

They had never suffered the *Lozi* before.

These creatures from the Isle of Lozan swam the river from the mainland, and swam the straits between the island and Macao, swam in the harbour from Kowloon to Hong Kong island itself. The junks and sampans, tiny craft and tramp steamers, were overturned into water seething with the *Lozi* who battened on to all food as it sank slowly through the sea.

The *Lozi* invaded the island of Hong Kong, and Kowloon in ever-increasing numbers, and soon terror filled the land of plenty.

It was as if, overnight, the population had become not four but forty million.

"He didn't mean it," the British Prime Minister said bitterly.
"The fools," said Copuscenti, hopelessly.
"What are the chances of stopping them?" asked the newspapermen who besieged 10, Downing Street.
"Is there any hope?" screamed the headlines.
"How many are there?" The Prime Minister demanded "Do you know, Palfrey? Tell me, do you know?"

In the awful week which followed the flight of the *Lozi* and the first of the famines, the truth of the extent of the invasion was brought home. The English colonies were small. The hordes of *Lozi* spreading over the famine areas could be calculated in hundreds of thousands, perhaps in millions, and there were dozens of such colonies.

The famine spread so fast that the horror was upon the whole of the Orient, and fear of famine struck at the heart of the West. A hurricane in Florida first hit the Keys and then Fort Lauderdale, missing Miami and Miami Beach in some miraculous way, but as the emergency kitchens were set up, and the help poured in from neighbouring states, the *Lozi* emerged from the swamps in the Everglades, from the reclaimed land itself, and fell upon the food. In panic a company of State Troopers released tear gas, which infuriated the *Lozi* but did them no harm. Another unit, of the marines, isolated hordes of the creatures on an island in the middle of Indian Creek, and used nerve gas. The effect on the *Lozi* was negligible but wind carried the gas up to Hollywood and whole residential areas were wiped out.

"I do not believe the figure at the end of the month can be less than a thousand million," Palfrey said to a conference of diplomats, a month after the first meeting. "I have now had the rate of increase estimated by the Family Planning Research Physicist. He confirms that in less than six months there will be no food left."

"Can we hold the position in Europe?" the German ambassador demanded. "We in Western Germany have already imposed strict food rationing."

"So have we," said France.

"We also," the Italian put in.

"We can last six months," the Dane reported.

"Four," said the Swede.

"Six weeks," said the Hungarian.

"Four," the Czechoslovakian reported.

So it went on, all over Europe.

In Washington, the Senate was in special session, and a senator from each state was ordered to report. Some were calm and resigned, some impassioned and angry, none could really believe the simple truth, and the truth was much the same as that in Europe.

"We have food supplies at subsistence level for twenty-one weeks," reported Connecticut. "And we know of large colonies of *Lozi.*"

"Twenty weeks," reported West Virginia. "And four colonies of *Lozi.*"

"Nine," said Washington. "And two."

"Twelve," reported Oregan, and the first hopeful note came next. "We have no known colonies of *Lozi.*"

"We can survive for nine months," boasted Texas. "We have the largest colony of *Lozi* in the world."

As the figures were reported, new reports came in, of efforts to contain the *Lozi,* by digging beneath their cities and pouring concrete into mammoth fissures so that the creatures could not tunnel through. But there was no way of stopping them coming over the top, and they were still more dangerous dead than alive. Their blood spread the infection further and further

All over the world armies and navies, air forces and civil defence groups worked like demons to contain the hordes, and all over the world the experts in chemical warfare and the experts in bacteriological warfare, and the research workers into nuclear power, and physicists and doctors, were striving without ceasing to try a gas or a poison which would kill the *Lozi* yet bring no harm to man.

Next they began to search for a method of killing the *Lozi* no matter what happened to mankind.

"And that looks like the beginning of the end," the British Prime Minister said to Palfrey.

In the past few weeks, he had become an old man, his hair nearly white, his face thin and deeply lined. He was at a window on the first floor of 10, Downing Street, looking along towards Whitehall. A silent crowd stood outside. Palfrey recalled his first meeting, the way Mason had reacted, not losing a moment. No one could blame him for what had happened and was about to happen, yet he shouldered all responsibility as if he blamed himself.

The people stared.

They too had aged, even the young seemed to have lined faces, and clothes which sagged about their bodies. Food rationing was so severe that none had more than one meal a day and for many the meal was insufficient. All the war time emergency measures had been put into effect; no one actually starved, but the day of starvation could not be far off.

"The beginning of the end," Mason repeated, in a hopeless voice. "Don't you agree, Palfrey? The only possible way to kill these brutes is to kill the people too."

Palfrey began to toy with his hair.

"It's the only way we can think of as yet," he remarked.

"There's so little time left," Mason said bitterly. "I have to go out soon, and speak to those people, and lie to them by giving them hope."

"Can that be a lie?" asked Palfrey, almost absently. The Prime Minister looked at him a little oddly. Palfrey smiled faintly in return. His cheeks were so thin that the bones showed sharply beneath an almost transparent skin. "I simply don't believe it, sir."

"Don't believe what?"

"That there's no hope."

"I didn't expect futile optimism from you," the Prime Minister said, then caught his breath. "No, I didn't mean that, Palfrey. I shouldn't have said it. You're the one man in the world who has never believed a single thing to be utterly impossible." After a pause, a look of expectation, faint, ready to be rebuffed, crept into his eyes. "You haven't grounds for hope, have you?"

"No," said Palfrey. "Not really. I'm going over to the Camp now."

"If there were any news from there, I would be told," said Mason. "I have a direct line." He gave a croak of laughter. "As if you didn't know. Have you noticed everybody is talking in clichés or repeating themselves over trifles? I've a direct line. Well!" He braced himself, and held out his hand.

Palfrey touched the bony fingers, which were icy cold.

"I'll keep you informed, sir."

"Do that," said Mason. Palfrey suspected that he was half-forgotten already, there was so much for this lonely man to do, too great a burden on his shoulders.

Joe Richardson, shrunk to a wraith, pathetic compared with his once great physical strength, opened the door for him. As they went downstairs, Palfrey heard that rare thing: a laugh. It was remarkable that laughter should sound so unusual, should appear to be almost wrong.

A door opened, and Beth came out. She was much thinner, yet still a fine woman, and the brightness of her eyes had not dimmed. It was characteristic of her that she was one of the few who had troubled to remodel her clothes, so that they fitted reasonably well.

"Thank you, Mrs. Fordham." The Prime Minister's wife came to the door, smiling. She looked at Palfrey. "Mrs. Fordham and I have just agreed that if you and James were the last two men alive, my husband would be making a policy speech to you, and you would be reproving him for considering the national and not the international implication of it."

Palfrey was startled into a chuckle.

"Beth," he said as they stepped outside of Number 10. "I don't believe there is another woman like you."

"There isn't another woman in the world like any other woman," Beth said off-handedly. She was still smiling, but the smile faded when she saw the silent, hopeless crowd in the street. Policemen whose uniforms sagged about almost fleshless bodies, whose helmet straps dangled almost to their chests, were watching the crowd listlessly. There was a path for vehicles in the middle of the street, and Palfrey and Beth walked along it, watched idly. There was a stir of interest as they neared Whitehall, and someone in a cracked voice shouted: "Listen!"

Palfrey paused, another voice sounded over a loudspeaker, recognisable as the Prime Minister's although very weak compared with the firm, resonant tone which had once captivated and fascinated tens of millions on television and radio.

"Ladies and Gentlemen," James Mason said, "I am grateful that so many of you have come here to support me at this time of great crisis. It is a great help indeed. And perhaps I can help you a little. We shall not need to make any further reductions in any of the basic food rations this week. In fact we may increase it a little next week, if the sugar beet crop in East Anglia is as good as we believe it might be. Meanwhile, every possible effort is being made to find a way of coping with the *Lozi*. In this age of great scientific and medical wonders, I for one simply do not believe that a way will not be found. The moment there is news, the moment there is hope, I will tell you."

As the voice faded a pathetic cheer arose, a desultory clapping. Palfrey and Beth moved on, a few others following them.

"Five minutes ago, he sounded absolutely hopeless," Palfrey said. "I've never known him so despairing. Remarkable how he can pep himself up."

"He's a remarkable man," Beth remarked. "Where are we going?"

"The Camp." "Must we?"

"I must. You needn't."

"Would you prefer me not to come ?"

Palfrey walked on a few steps in silence, and then turned to her, and said quite truthfully: "I am always less troubled when you are with me. You've given me a composure I haven't had for a long, long time. But I know you hate the Camp. Don't make yourself come."

She tucked her arm into his: "We'll walk through the park," she said.

They turned into the Horseguards, where only a few people stood and two guards, mounted on horses which looked too fragile to stand even their riders' light weight, stared unseeingly at parked vehicles which had become derelict. Only here and there did they see a moving car or taxi. Palfrey and Beth, walking quite quickly for their weak condition, but slowly in fact, neared St. James's Park and then Buckingham Palace. An uncanny silence reigned over London. On this bright, clear day, no one was in the park, the deck-chairs were empty, the flowers untended and bedraggled, the grass uncut. The few people in sight drooped, or shuffled along. There was a big crowd outside the palace, watching, waiting. Once each day the Queen came and spoke to her people, and still they waited.

"Did you realise what would happen?" Beth asked.

"The lassitude, you mean?"

"The fact that everything would stop."

"No," said Palfrey. "Not really. I should have, though. Food's the only fuel to create human power, and we simply can't work without it. A few slaves might, until they drop in their tracks, but not a society like ours. No one has the strength left to do anything. Everything has stopped."

And it was so. The factories and the farms were still. The life of the nation, of the world, had come to a standstill. All public work had stopped, save for a few basic necessities. There was no transport, in the air, on the ground, or below the surface. There were no great assemblies, no race meetings, no sporting gatherings. The theatres and the cinemas had closed. By superhuman effort, a programme was maintained on one television and one radio channel, and hospitals stayed open, although there was little they could do. The whole energy of the nation was concentrated on distributing the rations to the main food centres. Often, it took ten men to do the work of one. The schools were closed, but there was no sound of voices in the streets, for even the young were listless and subdued.

"Will they ever get it back?" Beth demanded.

"If we can find a way to feed them," Palfrey said simply, and then he laughed, remembering what the Prime Minister had said about triteness.

"Isn't that like you," Beth remarked, a wondering note in her voice.

"Whatis? Inanity?"'

"Nonsense, that wasn't inane. That was profound."

"Now, don't be absurd, Beth I—"

"Listen to me!" Beth interrupted, almost angrily for her. "How can you learn if you won't listen? Everyone else talks about killing the *Lozi,* you're almost the only one who ever thinks in terms of finding enough food for them. If there were enough for everyone and the *Lozi* it would be all right, wouldn't it?"

"Not quite all right," Palfrey said, mildly. "But better. Yes, better."

They walked past the side of Buckingham Palace, beneath the shadow of the Victory statue. The appalling irony was not that they should not kill but that they could not. As they crossed Hyde Park Corner, once a seething, noisy mass of traffic, a single small car driven by a grey-haired woman passed them. Just beyond was the one place which held the hopes of England, perhaps the hopes of the world.

It was now known as the *Camp of Lozi.*

Chapter Sixteen

THE CAMP OF *LOZI*

Before the mood of helpless despair had settled on the land, the Camp of *Lozi* had become known as the Camp. There were a few who felt bitter towards its very conception, because in a way it was so reminiscent of Belsen and Dachau, and similar concentration camps of ill-fame. This site, behind St. George's Hospital, had been selected because there was an extensive clearance and rebuilding scheme on foot, and London's councillors had extended the huge underground car park in Hyde Park so that it now covered – or would have, had the work been finished before the days of the famine – nearly a square mile. This had been selected as the Camp because the foundation, walls and ceilings were of reinforced concrete, and consequently the *Lozi* could not burrow their way out.

Under a crash programme, while men still had energy, and material was available, it had been divided into chambers and departments with fireproofed doors, electronically controlled, so they had been able to segregate certain groups of *Lozi*. The only major addition necessary had been observation windows of very thick glass. Part of this huge underground Camp had been equipped as a laboratory, and the whole of the resources of St. George's had been turned over to the desperately urgent work of research.

As they walked down the ramp towards the offices, Palfrey reflected ruefully on what Beth had said, and how right she was. All the equipment, all the research, all the efforts here, were devoted to finding ways of killing off the *Lozi,* not of the constructive task of growing more food. That was the pass to which society had been brought in this emergency. Looking back over his fifty-odd years, Palfrey saw with great bitterness, how true this was of society over the ages. *"Thou Shalt not Kill"* had been turned into the awful adage: *"How Best to Kill?"* Under the pressure of the invasion by *Lozi,* men of all nations had joined together, only to find that the awful weapons of destruction with which they had been prepared to destroy one another were useless.

Was it too late?

Had the years of blindness led mankind to the ultimate disaster – a means of being annihilated which they could not overcome? If nuclear research had always been for peaceful purposes, then Lozania would never have turned to the awful experiments which had created the *Lozi.* Now death would come in the way familiar to prehistoric man, to tribes, to cave-man communities: by starvation.

The oddest, in some ways the ultimate, bitterness was in the fact that in order to experiment on how to kill them, the *Lozi* had to be fed and kept in good health; for if they died of starvation here in the Camp, how could the chemists find means of destroying the countless millions now over-running the earth?

Palfrey said aloud: "I must stop moralising."

"You'll moralise to the day you die," said Beth, in her most matter-of-fact tone.

They reached the offices and Stefan Andromovitch came to meet them. He was leathery lean, and this made his great height even more noticeable. He had to duck beneath the doorways, and keep his head bent in the rooms. There was something a little reminiscent of Beth in his manner, in the gravity and yet the warmth of his smile. "Is there any special reason for your coming here?" he asked.

"Sap simply can't keep away and do nothing," Beth said.

"Every time I come I'm teased by the feeling that there's a solution, and it's staring us in the face." Palfrey said. "It's like a word on the tip of my tongue. Have you time to come round with us, Stefan?"

"Yes, of course."

They began to tour.

It was always the same, filling Palfrey with a sense of horror and yet hope. Here, at their most naked and malevolent worst, were the *Lozi*, pitiful little creatures when locked in, and, all but the fighters, helpless and harmless except for their voracious appetite. Some pressed tiny fingers and faces against the thick glass of the observation windows, some beat the glass with their beautifully-formed hands. None seemed to realise that they were breathing in gases and germs which would kill human beings.

No gas, no germ, had had as yet, the slightest effect.

They came to a large windowless laboratory, in the middle of these chambers, where several men were working, including Copuscenti. The physicist was one of the few men Palfrey knew who had not lost a great deal of weight, and the laboratory assistants were obviously better fed than most. When he saw Palfrey and Beth, Copuscenti raised his hands and lowered them slowly.

"Sap, it is wrong. *You* should not starve."

"I can manage on a lot less than I get," said Palfrey.

"I still say it is wrong. I cannot go on, eating my fill while you—"

"Nonsense!" Palfrey interrupted. "If we've any hope, it's from you. If you don't eat you can't work properly. Get that idea into your head. Is there any change?"

"None," said Copuscenti.

"None anywhere in the world," confirmed Andromovitch.

"Fire?" Palfrey made himself say.

"How can we burn them without burning ourselves?" demanded Copuscenti. "There are too many of them."

"Do they perish in flames?"

"Yes," Copuscenti said gruffly. "Yes." He took Palfrey's arm and led him to a chamber in a corner. As they approached it Palfrey saw the red hot glow inside, and felt the heat radiating even from the thick asbestos cover about it. Inside were bones ... "We have experimented fifty times," said the physicist. "They resist fire at ordinary temperatures, but a flame thrower—come."

He led the way again, to a small room, so crowded with the *Lozi* that for a moment Palfrey thought of the first time he had seen these little creatures as maggots. On the door was a note, saying: *A male and female were placed together here on August 7th. None has been added.*

It was October – and the room teemed with the tiny, human-like creatures. As Palfrey watched he saw some bread and potatoes fed into the room by some mechanical means. Immediately a surging mass of the *Lozi* appeared; struggling to get at the food, each eating as if ravenous. Fights broke out as those behind tried to push their way to the front.

Copuscenti said, "Watch."

He pressed a button, and a tongue of flame leapt out, straight at the mass of *Lozi* battening on the food. On that instant, a path was cleared; a hundred must have been burned to ash on contact with the flame. There were the burned and the blinded, reeling, writhing, mouths open as if screaming. Some died, as the others watched; and suddenly those who had not been injured surged forward over the charred remains, and fell upon the food and upon their dead fellows.

Beth said in a low pitched voice: "Oh God. It's awful."

"Human beings have always had cannibalistic tendencies," Copuscenti said. "Driven to desperation they have proved this countless times. But all the flame throwers in the world can't cover more than a few square miles. To try to destroy them this way would only drive them underground, and mean reducing the world on the surface to a molten hell." He was turning away from the chamber. "We have tried everything—everything."

"You see what this means, Sap," Andromovitch said. "These *Lozi* are proof against all known human ailments, against atomic radiation, against electricity and ordinary fire. Any amount of electric current can be passed through their bodies."

"I can demonstrate," Copuscenti said almost eagerly.

"No more demonstrations," Beth pleaded. "Sap, please take me away."

"Yes, Professor—has Dr. Walsh made any progress?"

"Only to prove that the infection is from contact with spilled blood, not from the breath," Copuscenti answered. "There is no further indication of the cause and no clue to immunisation."

Palfrey nodded and went from the Camp with Beth, leaving Copuscenti in the laboratory with the interminable round of experimental failures, and Andromovitch in the offices. They did not speak for a long time, until in fact they were near Green Park station. Palfrey remembered the way the *Lozi,* then unnamed, had attacked Baretta, and could recall the crowds of people suddenly appalled by what had struck at them out of the blue.

He saw a group of *Lozi* tearing at some tufts of grass in the park. No one else seemed to be aware of them. Hand firm on Beth's he went down in the lift. Here at last there was freedom from the creatures themselves, and what food there was would be safe from those sharp teeth and hungry bellies. Here was food stored against nuclear war and other emergency; at least those at the headquarters of Z5 would not starve.

There were two guards at the foot of the lift, as there were at each lift, to make sure no *Lozi* could escape.

"We'll be safe enough here when there's nowhere else to look after," Joyce Morgan said. She was coming out of her office as Palfrey and Beth approached, Beth to go along into a small apartment where she had been living for some weeks. Palfrey had an unhappy impression that these two women did not really like each other, but remained politely tolerant for his sake alone.

"I'll make some tea," Beth said.

"I'll be in the Operation Room," Palfrey told her.

This room, on the floor below his office, was a square almost empty chamber, with relief maps of the world round the walls, and a centre table supporting an enormous globe. Electronically operated, it could take reports from Z5 agents everywhere, and at the moment there was a clearing house for specific kinds of messages only. They had been carefully coded, and reception was automatic. There was no need for any operator in the room.

The numeral 1 meant: No change in situation.
The numeral 2 meant: No result from today's experiments.
The numeral 3 meant: *Lozi* have made no further advances.
The numeral 4 meant: Food stocks further reduced.
The numeral 5 meant: Famine conditions reached. Supplies desperately needed.
The numeral 6 meant: Medical help desperately needed.
The numeral 7 meant: Town or village or city, about to be evacuated.
The numeral 8 meant: Rioting out of control.
The numeral 9 meant: All inhabitants dead.
The numeral 10 meant: *Lozi* in complete control.

10, the ultimate despair.

Palfrey's agents still moved about the world as best they could, some used aircraft, some travelled by car, some on foot or by bicycle. Reports which had come in by the hundred when the cyphers had first been arranged, now came slowly, one at a time. In the East, district after district was illuminated by that numeral: 10. In Bombay, in Canton, in San Paolo, in Acapulca, in Alexandria, in a dozen other huge cities there was the nearly as ominous 8. Palfrey had learned to expect 9 to follow within days.

In some hill districts, particularly where there were thick rock strata, the *Lozi* had not made great inroads, and life was more or less normal except for lack of contact with the rest of the world. Radio and television, by Telstar and similar satellites, was now almost the only means of communication, and travel had stopped except for journeys by scientists and others who might be able to make some contribution to the solution of the problem. A few huge liners, stocked with canned and frozen foods, were at sea, but most of these were now in need of refuelling, few could cruise much longer. All of these showed 1 or 3. All without exception showed 4.

Now, Palfrey saw 5 – Famine Conditions reached – in a dozen new places, and with a fresh touch of horror he read this of vast expanses of the Argentine and of Australia, the granaries of the Western world.

Hungary showed two big areas, also at the point of famine. But of them all, the worst numeral was 10, which meant: *Lozi in complete control.*

The 10 glowed in most of the great plains and valleys of the East, in North Africa, in Arabia, in the Middle East, in South America, in the Deep South of the United States, over vast areas of Russia, on either side of the great European rivers, the Danube, the Volga, the Rhine, the Rhone. Wherever food grew most freely, there was the starkly horrifying: 10. It was dotted about the sugar producing areas of Queensland, Australia, Zululand, South Africa; it showed in all the river basins and in the reclaimed land of the world's oceans.

Whole islands were blank except for that dreadful 10.

The military and civilian authorities had been working at furious pressure for weeks, but the pressure had now slackened because of lack of food and, consequently, of stamina; but there were islands or oases of security in some parts of the world – like ghettos, with high walls and deep foundations, inside of which human beings crowded with their precious food stocks, surviving only because they were able to keep the *Lozi* out.

The food would not last long in any of these places; the moves to conserve it had started too late. There were millions upon millions of *Lozi,* doubling their number every other day, doubling their need for food which the world could not supply.

Palfrey was comparing numbers of the different countries with the figures of that morning, when the door opened and Beth came in, with tea.

Chapter Seventeen

THE IDEA

On the tea tray was a single, wafer-thin biscuit.

Joyce came in soon afterwards, and Beth picked up the biscuit and broke it into three pieces, of more or less equal size. Palfrey saw that Joyce's was perhaps slightly bigger, and he thought for a moment "That's not fair." He checked the thought. Beth poured tea. It was very watery; there was no milk, for most of the cattle were dead and the few which had survived yielded their meagre quantities for children. There was no sugar. Palfrey picked up his cup, and said: "Cheers."

They sipped.

"At least it's hot," said Joyce. "How long was the electricity on today?"

"Two hours," Beth answered. "There's no gas anywhere."

"How can we go on?" Joyce demanded, angrily. "I'm so hungry all the time I hardly know what to do. And look at me!" She slapped her stomach, taut and round with hunger's swelling.

Palfrey said "We'll go on while we can."

"It isn't worthwhile."

"While there's life there's hope," Beth said.

"Oh, that's kindergarten talk !"

"Out of the mouths of babes and sucklings," quoted Beth.

"Oh, you're insufferable!"

"I know, I must be," Beth conceded.

"You never complain."

"I don't see how complaining helps."

"You're so bloody smug!" Joyce said, her voice quivering.

"I'm just me," Beth said, simply.

"My God, you make me sick!"

"Joyce—" Palfrey began.

She swung round on him.

"Don't you start – you haven't anything to shout about."

"Would he shout if he had?" asked Beth, still equably.

"I tell you I can't stand it here! We're so powerless, helpless. *Look!*" Joyce pointed at the glowing figures, and as if at her command, two 10's leapt out of the darkness, close to Shanghai in South China, and Nagasaki in Japan. *"Look!"* she screamed again : "The *Lozi* have taken over there, they're everywhere, we haven't a hope of stopping them. And you sit there and spout platitudes!"

"Stop it, Joyce," Palfrey said sharply.

"I won't stop it, it's true. She's driving me mad!"

"Joyce—"

"Keep quiet!" screamed Joyce.

"Joyce," Palfrey said, his voice rising, "she gave you the biggest piece of biscuit."

"That's a lie!"

"It's the truth."

"She had the biggest piece."

"You did. I was watching."

The significance of what he had said struck home with savage hurtfulness, and Palfrey caught his breath. For a moment he thought that Joyce had been quietened, too, but she began again in the same shrill tone.

"Now you even watch every mouthful of food I take!"

"We all do."

"I don't. Don't you say I do. Don't ..." Joyce broke off. "I can't go on. I'm going to kill myself." She swung round and rushed out of the room, and Palfrey jumped to his feet. The sound of Joyce's footsteps echoed clearly at first, but gradually faded.

"I shouldn't follow her," Beth advised quietly.

"But she may kill herself."

"She won't," Beth said.

"You can't be sure."

Beth leaned across and took his hand. She actually smiled.

"No, I can't be," she admitted, "but I'm nearly sure, and if we go we might drive her to try, in defiance. It's best to leave her." After a pause, she went on: "Sap, when are you going to stop tormenting yourself? You can't live other people's lives for them. If she really wants to kill herself, then we can't stop her. I don't think she will. I don't think anyone screened by you and Z5 will ever take that way out, except to guard vital secrets. Do you?"

He stared into her eyes.

"Not really," he said slowly.

"Of course you don't," Beth said. "Sap—"

"Yes?"

"You've got to think."

"*Think?* What do you imagine I've been doing recently?"

"Reacting," Beth said quietly.

"*What?*"

"Reacting," Beth repeated firmly. "We all have. Everything has happened too fast for us, it's like being caught up in a torrent. We've been so busy keeping our heads above water we haven't really tried to swim." When Palfrey didn't answer, she went on: "You mustn't waste your energy on me, or Joyce, or Copuscenti, or the Prime Minister. You haven't enough to spare. Make your mind work as it's never worked before. Make your subconscious think."

He didn't answer but watched her, wondering what was in her mind; there were depths he hadn't plumbed, depths of which she herself was probably not aware.

"Sap," she went on. "You keep saying one thing over and over again."

"What thing?"

"That the solution to the problem is like a word on the tip of your tongue."

"That's so," he agreed.

"You seem so sure it's there."

"I feel sure."

"So, you have to probe your subconscious," Beth said. "But—" she broke off.

"Go on. Don't pull any punches."

"You won't let your mind concentrate on this problem only," she said. "You worry too much about individual pain. That way you'll never relax, or concentrate the way you always do best."

"And what way is that?"

"Single-mindedness," Beth said, and she gave a little laugh. "Expel me from your mind, expel Joyce, then, if there is a solution it will come to you in a flash. You know that, don't you?" When he didn't answer, she laughed again: "Look at you now!"

"What does that mean?" he hardly knew whether to be annoyed or amused.

"You're playing with your hair."

"I often do."

"Whenever you're preoccupied, yes. Do you know what I think?"

"Not at this moment."

"I think you play with your hair as if you were signalling to your subconscious," Beth declared. "Honestly, when you do it, do you consciously ponder anything? Or does your mind feel as blank as your face looks?" Again, quite spontaneously, Palfrey laughed.

"It feels blank enough," he admitted.

"There you are," said Beth with deep satisfaction. "I'm sure I'm right. You know your conscious mind goes blank and you call on the subconscious, and suddenly you get an idea – the solution to the problem which is baffling you."

Palfrey contemplated her very closely indeed. She was more excited than he had known her, and her eyes were very bright. She was earnest and yet half-laughing. He thought that loss of weight suited her, showing up the fine bone construction of her face; her lips particularly, were beautiful. He had an almost overwhelming temptation to take her in his arms; he had felt like that several times, but had not done so, and she seemed content with a friendship and an affection which lacked the fire of love. Now, however, something in his expression must have warned her what was going through his mind, and suddenly she sobered.

He said, with an answering sobriety: "Yes, you're right."

"Twist your hair round your finger and keep doing it," Beth ordered. "Keep doing it, Sap. *Make* your subconscious work."

Palfrey said: "I can only give it a chance to work."

"Do that then," urged Beth. "Do that."

Quite suddenly she moved forward, kissed him, hugged him, then walked silently out of the room.

While they had been talking, Smolensk in Russia, Calgary and Edmonton in Canada, Houston in Texas, Scottsbluff in Nebraska, Norwich in England, Cork in Ireland, Dijon and Grasse in France, Poznan in Poland, and seven other cities throughout the world flashed the dreaded 10.

The hordes of *Lozi* were sweeping all before them.

Palfrey sat at his desk, and tried to let his mind drift, but his thoughts kept coming back to the way Joyce had rushed out threatening to kill herself. It was futile to conjecture whether she would or not, as futile as the fierce argument had been. The remarkable thing was that all of them had kept their tempers for so long. But was Beth right?

Suddenly he jumped up.

"I'm going out to walk," he told the messenger on duty.

He went along to the lift and pressed the button, standing to one side as the door opened – and then fell back, his heart racing wildly as two of the killer *Lozi* streaked out, fur-clad devils which hurtled along the corridors and disappeared.

"Get them!" cried Palfrey. "Get them!" He raced down the passage to Beth's flat, and pushed the door open. "Careful !" he cried. "Two of the bloody things are in the place."

Beth turned to him, appalled.

"Lock yourself in," he ordered. "Don't come out until you're told that it's all clear."

It took an hour to locate the killer *Lozi,* and to trap them in a steel wire cage. Satisfied that that particular danger was over, Palfrey went along to reassure Beth, then took the lift up. On Piccadilly, the street was absolutely deserted, and he knew why; *Lozi* were about. He saw a pack of them in Green Park, mostly the ordinary creatures, but two were killers, attacking a skeleton thin Alsatian dog. They got it down and tore it to pieces. Palfrey turned away, sickened, and yet, by a terrible familiarity, hardened to horror.

Then he saw Joyce.

She was close to a gnarled tree, alone, watching the killer *Lozi.* Even at this distance, a hundred yards at least, Palfrey could see the terror in her eyes. He quickened his pace and walked towards her slipping a revolver from his pocket. Provided the blood was not touched, there would be no immediate danger. He did not call out, not wanting to distract the killers' attention. The earth usually so green, was barren, there was nothing gentle, or kindly, on which the eye could rest.

The killer *Lozi* turned away from the dog's bones, already stripped clean. They seemed to look at Joyce as if deliberating whether to attack her, but as they looked, and she shrank back against the tree, two other killer *Lozi* came from the houses bordering the park. Palfrey, gun levelled, prayed that there were no more.

He reached Joyce.

"It's all right," he whispered. "It's all right."

He put an arm round her, thinking wryly of the triteness and the emptiness of the words uttered. Then, surprised, he saw the two pairs of killer *Lozi* leap at *one another* in a savage battle which was obviously to be fought to the death.

Even then, the idea he was seeking did not come to him.

Joyce was quivering in his grip as he led her away, glancing behind him at that terrible scene, and seeing the more peaceful *Lozi* cowering away as if the fight terrified them, also.

"We'll go straight back," said Palfrey.

"Sap, I'm sorry."

"Forget it."

"I can't forget it. I'm terribly sorry."

"There's nothing to be sorry about."

"There is," Joyce said. "I know Beth's right for you. I know I made you get to know her better, but I'm still jealous. Sap, I'm so much in love with you."

Palfrey simply did not know what to say, so he gave her a little squeeze, and lengthened his stride.

"If we survive," said Joyce. "It is Beth who will have kept us sane. She's the woman for you, Sap. Even though half of me hates her, I know that's true."

"Joyce," he began, "you don't need—"

He broke off and swung round, for suddenly there was a squealing and groaning and yelping from the *Lozi,* and he thought for a dreadful moment that they were after him and Joyce. His finger was on the trigger, futile though he knew shooting would be if the pack's blood was up.

He did not shoot.

Two of the killer *Lozi* were attacking the ordinary ones with appalling savagery, and as some died, another pack of *Lozi* came racing towards those who were dead and dying, and began to tear them apart, and to devour them.

Joyce gasped : *"Look!"*

"My God," said Palfrey, in a choking voice. "That's it – that's what I've been after." Joyce stared at him but he did not appear to notice her, he was staring at the awful massacre taking place only a hundred yards away. "That's it," he repeated in a hoarse voice. "We can't destroy them, but they can destroy themselves."

Chapter Eighteen

NO OTHER HOPE?

Stefan Andromovitch sat in an enormous chair, facing Palfrey; once he had filled the chair, now there was room to spare. Professor Copuscenti walked about the big office, eyes glowing, cheeks flushed. Joyce, with notebook and pencil on her lap sat at a corner of the big desk, watching Palfrey with fixed intensity. Beth sat in an armchair, also watching Palfrey, a gleam in her eyes which might be of love, of compassion, or even of admiration. There was a kind of tension that had been missing for weeks, until Joyce suddenly exclaimed: "When on earth are they coming?"

As she finished there was a tap at the door, and it opened to admit the Rt. Honourable James Mason, the Prime Minister, and the Russian and American ambassadors. All three men came in falteringly, making the great effort needed for any kind of physical exertion. The grey-haired messenger and Stefan Andromovitch indicated chairs, and they sat down slowly, laboriously.

"Have you really some news for us?" the Prime Minister asked.

"I have what might be hope," Palfrey said.

"Is there anything more to ask for?"

"Don't keep us in suspense," Conlon added, in the thin tone of almost complete exhaustion.

"It is really very simple and yet very horrible," Palfrey said. "It has been there from the beginning, but we haven't seen it before." He paused, knowing how impatient the others were, and yet so tense himself that he was breathless; in fact he felt a mixture of excitement and of apprehension. Conlon was clenching and unclenching his hands in his lap; no one else moved at all. "There was an attack to the death by killer *Lozi* of one pack, on the killer *Lozi* of another pack, in Green Park two hours ago. The surviving killers then turned on the ordinary *Lozi,* and their pack ate them."

The Prime Minister caught his breath.

"Ate?" echoed Conlon.

"So. They are cannibals," said Halik. "Of course there has been evidence before – when they cannot get normal food, they will feed off their own kind."

"I still don't understand," said Conlon. "I would have thought it likely to spread the disease. How can it help?"

"When there's no other food they will turn on each other." Palfrey said. "We have to make doubly sure they can't get at our food stocks. We have to reinforce all of our towns and cities, all the centres where there is still food. Then we have to make absolutely sure none of the *Lozi* can feed off the surrounding land, as they are doing now. When there is absolutely no food left, they will turn on each other."

"Can you be sure?" demanded Conlon.

"I think we can make sure," Palfrey said.

"Think!" urged Copuscenti. *"Think,* for the love of God."

"We haven't attempted to kill them in large numbers for fear of too much blood-letting, and the consequent radiation through contact," Palfrey said. "But if they turn on each other, though blood-letting will be inevitable, human contact with it need not be. If we call in as many people as we can and they are compelled to stay inside germ-proof centres, they will be in little danger of poisoning."

Halik said heavily: "No one must be outside such centres if they are to be effective. What little harvesting is being done will have to stop. All small food centres will have to be closed. Here in England it is possible. It will not be so in Russia."

"Or in the United States," Conlon interpolated. "The distances are too great. Even with the normal means of distribution available it would be impossible to move all food stocks. And when one begins to think in terms of India and China—" he broke off, passing his hand against his forehead.

Palfrey could imagine exactly how he was feeling; knew that he was afraid to face the sacrifices that any effective hope would make inevitable. The Prime Minister was leaning back with his eyes closed, and when he spoke it was in the cracked voice of an almost dying man.

"Even in England, we cannot save everybody. The death rate today is twice as high as normal. In India, it is four times the normal rate, so—whatever we do cannot save everybody. What is really in your mind Palfrey?"

Palfrey answered very carefully: "Selective sacrifice, sir."

"Be more explicit, please."

Palfrey leaned forward, looking at the three men in turn, and when he spoke he weighed his words with even greater care.

"I will try to be more explicit. As the situation now stands, there is no hope for mankind, because there is not enough food to supply human beings and the sub-human *Lozi*. We are agreed about that, I am sure."

Halik nodded, the Prime Minister said, "Yes", Conlon muttered, "I guess so."

"It is doubtful whether any human beings will survive for more than six months, because all the food which can be grown will be gone, and there will be no one left with the strength to till the land and plant the seeds. As things are, this is our last year of harvest."

"I hate to admit it," Conlon said, "but you are right."

"So anything which offers an improvement must be accepted," reasoned Palfrey.

"Go on," Halik said.

"If we draw a pre-determined number of people into the protected food centres, those people can live indefinitely – certainly until the *Lozi* outside turn and devour each other."

"Yes," agreed the Prime Minister, "always provided we don't try to keep too many people in the centres. Isn't that your point?"

"It is," said Palfrey simply. "There is enough food for a certain number of human beings. There is no way of keeping the others alive. The facts, as far as I can judge, are that the food stocks in the main centres are sufficient to save ten per cent of the people now living in those centres."

Conlon almost groaned: "Ten *per cent.*"

"Is that all?" asked the Prime Minister, wearily.

"It is not likely to be higher than twelve per cent."

Halik shifted forward in his chair.

"So the others must die?"

"They will die in any case," put in Andromovitch. "There is no hope for any of us unless we do what Palfrey suggests."

"Precisely what do you advise?" asked Conlon in a tense voice.

"As I see the situation, sir, ten per cent of the people in all the centres must be protected, but the others sacrificed," said Palfrey. "We must save a cross-section of mankind. Age will be a major, but not the only, factor. We must make a selection of wise, clever and experienced people of all ages and in all spheres of life, from the professions, from commerce, industry, and agriculture. After that, we must select the adults most likely to preserve the world's civilisation at its best. In effect, we must sacrifice all the people beyond the age of forty. If we take a rough figure, by making the age thirty-five, we will have ruled out two-thirds of the world's population. We can then save a third of those who are left. They too would have to be carefully selected for physical and intellectual fitness."

"It is just not possible," Conlon said, hoarsely.

"Who would make such a selection?" demanded Halik.

"That's the horror of it," said the Prime Minister. "Who can take such a responsibility ? Some means of natural selection would be essential."

Into a tense silence Andromovitch said: "There is no natural selection except the survival of the fittest, and unless we make an arbitrary choice even the fittest will have little chance of surviving. That much is obvious. A selection must be imposed."

"You haven't answered my questions: by whom?" The Prime Minister's eyes were so heavy with pain it was hurtful even to look at him. "Have you worked that out, Palfrey?"

"Yes," said Palfrey quietly.

"Tell us."

"Every city and centre has its administrative leaders, its Emergency Committee," Palfrey said. "Each leader will have to make its own selection. It cannot be done by debate or discussion in committee. Stefan is quite right when he says that it must be an arbitrary choice. The chairmen have all been carefuly chosen and appointed because of their especial qualifications to lead in an emergency. Every one of them must be visited, or sent a coded cable. That can be done by each country from its capital."

"How can you be sure all governments will agree?"

"We can't," Palfrey admitted. "But when they face the facts of the situation, I think they will. First, we need another meeting of ambassadors. If you three gentlemen will support my recommendations I will brief each one, who will in turn return to his capital to brief his own government. Each capital will then call an emergency meeting of military and civil leaders in the various centres. There will be at least one such meeting in each State of America, for instance, and in each Russian Republic. The military and civil leaders will be carefully briefed, and it is they who will call a meeting of all the leaders of the centres, large and small."

"But this will take weeks!" protested the Prime Minister.

"I think two weeks," answered Palfrey. "And another two will be needed to organise the exodus from each centre."

"You've forgotten one vital thing," Halik declared.

"Have I, sir?"

"Yes. The people won't leave the centres."

"They will if they are persuaded that they are migrating to an area free from the *Lozi*" Palfrey said.

"How can one—"

Andromovitch stood up abruptly, moved across to the desk and stood behind Palfrey's chair. He towered above them all, and there was nothing saint-like, now, in his expression, only anger and strength.

"Do what you wish," he said roughly. "Go and pretend the *Lozi* don't exist. Wait until the world is dead around you, and death takes you yourselves."

"Now, Andromovitch—" Halik began.

"All my life I have been working with Palfrey to try to make politicians and statesmen see the elementary truths," Andromovitch went on, "and the result is always the same. Obstruction, obstruction, obstruction. 'Let everyone else do his duty, don't expect it of me.' For three thousand years men have strangled one another because they haven't had the sense to see the obvious. We have had war after war, emergency after emergency because politicians stick their heads in the sand. My God, I am sick of it, sick of you. Palfrey and I and a few hundred others have worked ceaselessly trying to reason with fools who will not see what they don't want to see. But for him, but for us, there would be no world left. Have you ever paused to think about that? Have you ever stopped thinking about yourselves and your nation's problems, to consider what would have happened if a few disinterested, selfless individuals, had not sacrificed everything, to make you come to terms with reason? I know one thing. If you are truly representative, the world doesn't deserve to survive. We would be better if mankind was wiped off the face of the earth."

He stopped abruptly. He was quivering with the nervous energy expended in the outburst and the attempt to control his anger. He put a hand on Palfrey's shoulder as he went on: "This man has wisdom, compassion, courage and intelligence. Do what he says and you will preserve the world, and our civilisation, our cultures, everything we have won in these thousands of years. Ignore him, argue and delay, and it will all be gone."

He took his hand from Palfrey's shoulder, glared at the diplomats, then crossed the room and stalked out.

Into the hushed silence which followed, Conlon said: "I think you should call the meeting of ambassadors, Palfrey."

"Quickly," said Halik.

"I can arrange it," the Prime Minister promised. "It is eleven o'clock now. I will have them at the Assembly Room by four o'clock this afternoon."

"Can you have the briefing ready by then?" asked Conlon.

"It is ready," Palfrey said.

One after another, they went out, leaving Palfrey with Beth and Joyce. He had hardly stirred since Andromovitch had started on his harangue, and there was a shocked expression on his face, as if he could not believe what he had heard. Joyce stood up, and moved to him; he looked up at her.

"Stefan was right," she said. "Absolutely right." She bent down and touched his forehead with her lips, then turned and went out, without glancing at Beth.

Palfrey stared straight ahead of him.

Beth moved, so that she was in his line of vision. She smiled at him, and he looked up. She saw the pain, the anguish in his eyes. He wondered in a strange half-world of torment whether she even began to understand what he felt now.

"Sap," Beth said, "you're looking at it in the wrong way."

His lips moved. "Am I?"

"You are thinking of the millions you will send to their death."

He caught his breath.

"But you should be thinking of the millions you are saving from the death which the folly of others brought near," Beth said. "*You* aren't sending or condemning anyone, the world has done that by its follies, *you* are saving millions. In a few short hours you can have the whole plan prepared, you can put it into immediate action. They will do it, Sap. They will have to because there is no other hope. And it will succeed."

He muttered: "I pray that it will."

"Many millions of lives will be saved, our civilisation will be preserved, and all the good things in it," insisted Beth. "There's even a possibility that many of the bad things and the folly will be purged. And all of this because of one man, because of you." As she finished, he stood up.

They moved together, and Palfrey felt a peace he had not known in many years, the peace only a woman he loved and who loved him could bring. Yet they did not speak of love.

Chapter Nineteen

THE SACRIFICES

The ambassadors foregathered.

Outside, newspaper, radio and television reporters, recorders and cameras, were trained on the doorway of the great building in Whitehall. As the cars drew up, or the ambassadors arrived on foot, the silent crowd observed them with a resigned hopelessness. Policemen were mixing freely with the crowd, and dozens of Palfrey's men were present, listening to rumours and talk. There was a spirit of defeatism. Now and again, *Lozi* streaked past, and no one took any notice of them; only the killer *Lozi* would attack humans, and none of those appeared.

When the Prime Minister arrived, he mounted the steps and spoke into a B.B.C. microphone.

"I will have a statement for you when I come out. At this stage I can say no more."

There was a faint stirring of interest, but no glimmer of excitement. Soon the ambassadors were behind locked doors. This time there was neither food nor drink for them.

Palfrey began to talk, bringing his audience through an atmosphere of stunned horror, growing restlessness, and gradual hope. He outlined the plan anew, as he had outlined it to the three men in his office, then he said clearly and precisely: "We have made tape-recordings of these plans, two for each of you. It wouldn't be wise to put them on paper. The stages are carefully graduated – if the instructions are carried out, there is little need to fear failure, because I have here—" he held a sheet of paper above his head—"a list of twenty-one proved instances of cannibalism among the *Lozi*. When they are starving, they will eat one another. We need time. We need preparation-and-food centres which are impregnable; and we need patience."

He paused but soon went on: "Before I invite your questioning, there is one matter of vital importance. That of the effect on the people whom we are going to sacrifice. They will be told, all of them, that they are heading for other food centres, where there is more chance of survival than in the one they leave. They will be given military protection – among those whom we shall send out will be many of military age. It will be like the Exodus from Egypt, for they will leave in hope. I believe you will understand that we are not dooming them, for the world as it stands is already doomed. We are snatching at the one slender chance of a future for mankind."

He stopped.

For a while, no one spoke.

Then one man began to pray, and others followed him.

So complete was their agreement that no one argued, nor protested, nor demurred.

Outside, in Whitehall, the Prime Minister put up the remarkable front which never seemed to desert him, and his voice was strong and sure as he lied.

"We have realised that the cities and towns cannot be properly protected unless there are fewer people in them. And we realise also that the *Lozi* will invade the cities and the towns, and the disease of radiation will spread much more quickly along the sewers and the gutters of built-up areas. Safety, therefore, depends on an organised exodus to places in the country which have already been prepared, and there food supplies are being accumulated.

"A selected few will stay behind in the cities and the towns, to protect the marching columns from attack from the rear.

"There need be no panic. It must be an orderly exodus, we must not regard ourselves as refugees. Remember, this is the policy which will be applied throughout the world – the east and the west, the new world and the old.

"And we begin tomorrow."

In his last remark the Prime Minister was wrong. They began within moments of the last words of his speech. In the homes throughout the land where they had heard him, many began to prepare. They collected oddments of clothing and furniture, their personal as well as their household treasures, and they started the trek out of the city.

And others began throughout the world.

There was no need to send military forces with them, no need to bribe or persuade. Enough of the refugees were on the way to make certain that the selected survivors would have no need to fear. Soon the streets were thronged. Every kind of wheeled vehicle which could be pushed or pulled was used, push-carts and hand-trucks, bicycles, tricycles and prams. And as the hordes moved out, the leaders of the Emergency Committees worked with desperate intensity to keep those whom they wanted behind, until Andromovitch said: "Those who wish to go should be allowed to, Sap. They haven't the qualities which the survivors will need if we are to rebuild the world."

There was profound truth in that, and Palfrey sent out the message, and the leaders heeded.

All day, all night, all day, all night, the people left the cities and the towns and spread over the countrysides of the world, while the *Lozi* watched, and the killer *Lozi* prowled, as puzzled by human behaviour as humans had been by theirs.

Night followed night, and day followed day, until the city streets were deserted, and there were only the people of the future waiting.

In West Pakistan, where the famine conditions had been among the most acute, there was nothing left for man or *Lozi*. In Lahore, in a corner of the Shalimar Gardens where the flowers were dead and the fountains idle, two packs of *Lozi* appeared, with killers at their heads. An old gardener, who had somehow survived, squatted cross-legged by a wall, his goat skin water carrier empty, his face that of a skeleton, his body skin and bones. He saw the killers of one side sidle up to the killers of another, heard the screeching and squawking and saw the furious fight to the death.

From all over the world, the reports came in.

As the great packs became hungry, they fought each other, and this happened time and time again outside the cities. The armies of human beings, without food, without water, were thinned out as first one and then another dropped in his tracks. The scarecrow millions, their sunken faces telling of the nearness of death, lost all hope, or desire for it. And as they came upon the places where the *Lozi* had fought, the sickness came upon them, and they died.

The soil died too.

In the cities and the towns, reports came in from sputniks and television, and from view reconnaissance rocket planes which were in continual flight, sending pictures back to earth.

In all the capital cities, the leaders of nations saw what was happening, and were appalled.

On the screen at the headquarters of Z5, Palfrey and Andromovitch, Joyce and Beth, saw how the hopeless masses dropped and starved and fell sick and died; saw how the *Lozi* fell upon one another, and when one pack emerged triumphant, how it ran over the earth in its never ending search for more food. And in some packs the young were born and so the population rate increased, but in other packs hunger reduced the number until it was clear at last that the *Lozi* population was declining all over the world.

The time came when the *Lozi* protecting a pack turned on those it was protecting.

That was the beginning of the end.

For a long time after that the *Lozi* survived and in places thrived, but never for very long. Soon, the earth was running with the thin, watery blood which seeped into the soil, and killed all the vegetation that was left. Whole forests fell as disease struck at their roots. The sparse vegetation of the deserts faded, the more luxuriant vegetation of the jungle withered, and to the observers it began to look as if all growth was stunted by the bloodbath of the *Lozi*. No one stirred from the cities, where the food stocks fell lower and lower. Here and there the food was used up, and the hopelessness of famine drove the people away to scavenge over the poisoned earth for anything which might keep them alive.

Few found it! Fewer survived.

"One thing is certain," Andromovitch said to Palfrey. "No one would be alive now, but for the centres. It was the only possible way, Sap, if there is to be a new world."

Palfrey felt Beth's hand upon his arm, but the ache of guilt was acute in him. He could not forget that at his behest, the millions had gone to die, and that there was no certainty of survival for those that remained. Day after day the news was the same, and day after day some city fell to rioting, to looting, and some of those who had stayed behind broke out to seek nourishment which did not exist, and died.

Each day, samples of the poisoned earth were brought into laboratories in all the big cities, and tests were run, in the desperate hope that the scope and malignancy of the disease were weakening; for the terror now was not whether they could grow food enough, but whether they could grow food at all.

"How long will we survive in London?" Joyce asked, in the eleventh week.

"Perhaps another four months."

"We can't grow anything in four months."

"We could grow the simpler crops," said Palfrey. "Most of the root vegetables, all the salad vegetables, beans and peas. We could survive if—"

He broke off.

That was how the conversation ran these days; in fits and starts. No discussion ever seemed to get anywhere, few sentences were finished. Of the little group of survivors at Z5, Beth was the least affected, having, perhaps, more spiritual stability.

Each saw their physical strength dwindling.

They began to lose the will to live.

And then one day, there came a messenger from Lozania.

The son of Clemente Taza came without warning to Z5. He was admitted by the guard at the main lift, and was conducted along the silent passages to meet Palfrey. Palfrey was with Andromovitch in the big office. He remembered, as from another life, the first time he had seen this man's father at the early conference of ambassadors; and he remembered the shot with which President Montini had killed himself, unable to live with so deep a sense of guilt.

Young Taza, however, appeared untouched by culpability.

"Dr. Palfrey," he said. "I have an eight millimetre film to show you, from the Isle of Lozan. Have you the facilities here?"

"Of course."

Palfrey was not only too listless to think seriously, he was too listless to wonder what this was about. For days, now, it had been simply a matter of survival, of hanging on, without any sense of time or urgency.

At last the room was darkened, and a picture appeared on the screen of the barren rocky soil of the island after the explosion which had created the *Lozi*. The whirring of the camera had a soporific effect; and Palfrey found himself drifting into a state of semi-consciousness.

He was brought back to the scene by a change of picture. Over the dark barren sides of the island there appeared a faint green film. Gradually it darkened, and more vegetation appeared. As the projector whirred on, the son of Clemente Taza spoke: "These pictures were taken every twenty-four hours – one each day."

There was a break in the film, and then suddenly the screen showed vivid green and much more luxuriant growth.

"That in one day?" demanded Andromovitch, incredulously.

"That is so," asserted Taza, "but I ask you to wait, please."

Now Palfrey was sitting upright, the blood running less feebly through his veins, and when the next picture flashed on, he exclaimed aloud, for now he could see the shape of trees as well as bushes, grass, and wheat, all mixed together. With increasing excitement still touched by disbelief, he saw crops grow as much in days as they had once grown in weeks. "You will see what has happened," young Taza said, in a flat unemotional voice. The rate of reproduction was speeded up in animal life. The rate of germination and growth has speeded up in vegetable life. All of this land was fertilised by the blood of *Lozi,* Dr. Palfrey. The rest of the earth should begin to bear fruit. We know already that it is clean; no one has been attacked by the disease in more than a week."

And it was so.

As the days passed, a miracle came upon the world. Seeds long buried in that soil which had been poisoned for so long germinated, and grew so quickly that the tired and starving humans could scarcely believe it. Within two weeks, the first root crops were being harvested, excitement and hope giving the people strength to labour; within two more, the first corn and wheat and rice followed. All over the world food began to grow, and as the people ate they grew in stature and happiness, filled with a forgotten zest for life. In India and in China, in the once barren lands, in deserts or in valleys the food crops flourished. And of the people, none was sick.

Chapter Twenty

IN THE BEGINNING ...

Palfrey and Beth stepped out of a car beneath an oak tree in a narrow lane which led from the gaunt Goose Inn a mile or so away. The hedges, like the oak, were bursting with new life, a fresh and beautiful green. They stood for a few moments by the side of the car, watching the rippling of the corn beneath the evening breeze.

The five-barred gate had been repaired and painted, and they reached it and leaned against it, Beth watching the rippling of the corn with the intensity which Palfrey had seen in her from the first. He could recall, as she could not, her expression when she had looked down at her dead husband, the second victim of the *Lozi.* He could remember how she had told him what she had seen, and her tone as she approached the full horror.

"Do you want to go into the field?" asked Palfrey.

"Yes, Sap, please."

He opened the gate, and they walked along the verge where the grass grew and the corn stalks bent to the breeze. The combine-harvester had been taken away, and the city of the *Lozi* had been filled in. There was no more to mark it than a dip in the ground. It was a year since Palfrey had first walked, in near panic, across this field, and yet it was an age ago. At this moment he felt something of the horror he had known here, the sense of the unknown, brooding menace. Nothing would ever drive that memory, or the fear, away. As he watched the sunlight and shadow, he could imagine the millions who had walked out so hopefully and so bravely to their death.

"Sap," Beth said.

"Yes, my dear."

"Don't torture yourself."

He smiled at her. "How do you do it?" he demanded wonderingly. "You sense every mood, almost every thought. I've never known anyone like you."

Slowly, Beth asked: "Not even Drusilla?"

"Not even Drusilla."

Just for an instant pain showed in the blue eyes, as memories of the young wife who had died so tragically came crowding back to him – but it was quickly veiled.

"You would have liked her." He paused for a moment, then put a friendly hand on Beth's shoulder. "Do you ever think of David?"

"It's strange," said Beth dreamily. "He was a simple man but there was a very great quality in him. An honesty, a forthrightness. He was a farmer, and he saw farmers' problems as you see mankind's. You are both so unbelievably different, yet you are both so alike. He used to worry about a neighbour's crop after a storm much more than he did about his own. I don't think I ever told you that he would have harvested this field three days earlier had he not helped a neighbour whose wife was sick. And you came here because the world was sick. Do you think it has healed itself, Sap?"

Palfrey stared at her, and began to twist a few hairs round his forefinger.

"Not yet," he said. "But we might heal ourselves eventually. There's enough of everything to go round now, we won't have to fight to get a fair share. We've inherited the technical know-how, the medical and surgical know-how, the culture, even the philosophy and the common sense, of two thousand and more years. The question is, have we inherited the greed and the folly as well? If we go about it in the right way, it will be like being born without ever having to be young. We start with all the advantages of experience and knowledge. Oh, we've a chance."

He stopped speaking.

He patted the strand of hair down onto his forehead into a flaxen curve.

"I think today's children will be born with a much greater chance than children in the past. I suppose we shouldn't ask more."

"No," Beth said. "It is enough."

They turned, their hands linked, and walked back through the new growth to a new life, which only mankind could ever spoil.

JOHN CREASEY

GIDEON'S DAY

Gideon's day is a busy one. He balances family commitments with solving a series of seemingly unrelated crimes from which a plot nonetheless evolves and a mystery is solved.

One of the most senior officers within Scotland Yard, George Gideon's crime solving abilities are in the finest traditions of London's world famous police headquarters. His analytical brain and sense of fairness is respected by colleagues and villains alike.

'The finest of all Scotland Yard series' – New York Times.

GIDEON'S FIRE

Commander George Gideon of Scotland Yard has to deal successively with news of a mass murderer, a depraved maniac, and the deaths of a family in an arson attack on an old building south of the river. This leaves little time for the crisis developing at home ....

'Gideon of Scotland Yard emerges as one of the most real working detectives in modern fiction.... A sympathetic and believable professional policeman.' - New York Times

JOHN CREASEY

THE CREEPERS

"The prisoner's hand was thin and bony ... And in the centre of the palm was a pinkish mark. It was the shape of a wolf's head, mouth open, fangs showing. Although it was what he had expected to see, Inspector West felt a twinge of repugnance a stab not unrelated to fear. It was the fifth time he had seen the mark of the wolf – the mark of Lobo."

A gang of cat burglars led by Lobo cause mayhem as they terrorize the city. They must be stopped, but with little in the way of evidence the police are baffled. Just how can Inspector West manage to do this in what is a race against time before more victims succumb?

"Here is an excellent novel of law enforcement officers, harried, discouraged and desperately fatigued, moving inexorably ahead under the pressure of knowledge that they must succeed to save human lives." - Cleveland Plain-Dealer

"Furiously exciting" - Chicago Tribune

"The action is fast, continuous and exciting" - San Francisco News

John Creasey

Introducing the Toff

Whilst returning home from a cricket match at his father's country home, the Honourable Richard Rollison - alias The Toff - comes across an accident which proves to be a mystery. As he delves deeper into the matter with his usual perseverance and thoroughness , murder and suspense form the backdrop to a fast moving and exciting adventure.

'The Toff has been promoted to a place of honour among amateur detectives.' – The Times Literary Supplement

Case Against Paul Raeburn

Chief Inspector Roger West has been watching and waiting for over two years – he is determined to catch Paul Raeburn out. The millionaire racketeer may have made a mistake, following the killing of a small time crook.

Can the ace detective triumph over the evil Raeburn in what are very difficult circumstances? This cannot be assumed as not eveything, it would seem, is as simple as it first appears .....

'Creasey can drive a narrative along like nobody's business ... ingenious plot ... interesting background .' - The Sunday Times

11371812R00094

Printed in Great Britain
by Amazon.co.uk, Ltd.,
Marston Gate.